THE GUNS
OF
TERRA 10

by

Don Pendleton

Dedication

For Rod, and for all the

conscious men.

All forms of tampering with human beings, getting at them, shaping them against their will . . . is, therefore, a denial of that in men which makes them men.
—Sir Isaiah Berlin

The danger of the past was that men became slaves. The danger of the future is that men may become robots.
—Erich Fromm

We must, however, acknowledge, as it seems to me, that man with all his noble qualities . . . still bears in his bodily frame the indelible stamp of his lowly origin.
—Charles Darwin

CHAPTER ONE

The Big Gamble

A trickling chill shivered through his six-and-a-half foot frame, causing Gunner Zach Whaleman to pause momentarily on the porch outside Board Central. He shook off the weird sense of alarm and gazed down on the brilliantly lighted grounds and the artificial grass and flowers which concealed the ugly black sands of Board Island. The volcanic island in the Central Atlantic could have been on any of the dead planets, he was thinking, except for the dense atmosphere and the pleasant environmental conditions. There was little about Board Island to remind a man of his Terran roots. Grim and bleak, just as most other places in the solar system, there was nothing here of sweet scents and exhilarating landscapes which made the earth stand unique in the solar scheme. Whaleman quickly descended the steps and angled across the synthetic turf toward the parking area.

A pretty GovTech stepped out of an intersecting walkway, smiled hesitantly at the big Gunner, then quickly approached. He recognized her intent and slowed his pace to allow the interception.

The girl was petitely human, fully two feet shorter than Whaleman, but shapely and appealing in the GovTech gray.

"Well done, Gunner," she greeted him. "I saw your shooting. Do you stay at Board Island tonight?"

Another chill traversed the Gunner's frame. Again he dismissed it and bent to receive a kiss on the cheek. It was a social gesture, completely lacking in erotic undertones. "I am not yet decided," he replied coolly.

"My quarters are available for sexual companionship," she informed him.

He touched hands with her and said, "Apology, I am not yet decided."

The girl smiled, the usual lip-twister of the homans. "Billet 7 Berth 64, if you decide."

Whaleman jerked his head lightly to the left in a terse salute and went on his way. He realized that the girl was simply being hospitable. Homan females were not generally attracted to Defense Commanders, and vice versa. Whaleman preferred the more bountiful charms of Defense Command females. He supposed it to be a matter of genes, dismissed the girl from his mind, and turned into the parking station.

His gravcar was one of only about a dozen remaining, and he was more than a little surprised to find it surrounded by a party of Defense Commanders. The hatch stood open and a blond giant was seated at the controls. Whaleman hastened his pace, a strange feeling beginning at the pit of his stomach. His first thought was that a crew from one of the cruisers selected to tow Terra 10 was awaiting him, and he could think of no reason why they should do so. Was there a glitch in the schedule?

A huge Commander with spaceblack hair stepped forward to greet Whaleman. Some indefinable strangeness of the man's uniform intensified the curling of the Gunner's stomach.

"Ho, Gunner," the odd-looking commander greeted him.

Whaleman touched hands with him and immediately knew another strangeness. The man's hand was steely hard, tight and rough to the touch. The voice also possessed a timbre that was totally alien to Defense Commanders. It was deep, resonant, almost musical. Whaleman stiffened.

"Identity," he demanded.

The others were forming a loose circle about them. The dark man laughed and said, "I'm Tom Cole, King of the Reevers."

Whaleman's first impulse was to smile at an obvious joke, but the smile came as a frozen grimace. The man was not joking. The blond man poked his head through the open hatch of the gravcar and announced, "Hey, Tom, I've got the thing figured out. I can fly'er."

The words came as a musical blur to Zach Whaleman. Even so, his worst fears were realized.

"Reevers!" he spat disgustedly. "Why in uniform of Defense Command? Why on corporate grounds?" He shoved the dark giant aside and strode angrily toward the gravcar.

"Take him!" Tom Cole thundered, and then the unbelievable occurred. A Gunner of the Defense Command was physically attacked by an idiot band of Reevers.

A hard fist in his belly doubled Whaleman over at the waist and another smashing blow to the head sat him down. He gazed dully around, trying to understand the astounding attack. Then a long-dormant instinct, which not even genetic manipulation could completely destroy, took charge of the Gunner's body, and he scrambled to his feet with an angry bellow, lashing out at his attackers with murderous sweeps of his big arms. Two of the Reevers were sent rolling across the synturf and another was chopped to the ground before Whaleman was overcome and borne down by the weight of determined numbers. Tom Cole stepped into the pile-up and delivered a stunning blow to the Gunner's chin. He stopped fighting then, and was hauled to his feet and hustled into the gravcar.

The Reever leader roughly shoved the Gunner into a rear seat, pinning him in between two other men. The others quickly climbed in, and the car rose jerkily into the air.

The big blond chuckled as he bent tensely over the controls.

"Not bad for a stupid-ass mental deficient, eh?" he crowed triumphantly.

The gravcar pitched about and began slipping away toward the west in a sharply crabbing attitude. The driver made a correction, and they levelled into a smooth acceleration.

"Do that again, Hedge, and I'll throw up," a man said shakily.

"Leave 'im alone, he's doing fine," Tom Cole rumbled from the middle row of seats. He swivelled about to regard his prisoner with a hard stare. "You're quite a fighter," he said admiringly.

Whaleman understood none of the rushing gibberish, the words impacting his mind as a meaningless blur. He was dazed and, for the first time in his memory, frightened.

"Request slow speak," he said thickly.

The big Reever exploded into laughter. "You gotta talk like robots, boys, if you want to get through to this superguy. For Mars' sake, don't talk like men!"

His companions joined in with gleeful comments, and the man seated to Whaleman's right playfully slapped the Gunner's knee and gave him a reassuring smile. But none of them addressed Whaleman directly throughout the remainder of the trip to North America. They skimmed along barely above the heaving Atlantic, and Whaleman tried to relax as the hurtling gravcar maneuvered wildly around hovering sea-harvesters and automated ocean stations. Occasionally, he would see shimmering blobs beneath the waters, which could only be the mammoth floor-crawlers. Then they were flashing over green fields and majestic orchards, and the untutored pilot was cautiously increasing their altitude.

A strip city appeared momentarily as a horizon-to-horizon unbroken line of brilliant structures, then instantly disappeared from view as they swept past and dropped to a tree-skimming level. Whaleman held his breath and hoped that the driver knew the terrain well as they hurtled on just above the treetops at quadrasonic speed.

A moment later, they were braking into a jarring slowdown and the gravcar was going into a lateral spin. One of the Reevers yelled something unintelligible, and the blond man was jerking at the stabilizer.

Whaleman released his constricted lungs and glanced down toward the ground. They were descending slowly now, in good control, and settling gently into a small clearing in the trees. Plastic huts with domed roofs ringed the clearing, from which near-naked people were erupting and running excitedly about in the open area.

The dark giant with the black hair leaned over his seat and touched Whaleman lightly on the chin.

"We mean you no harm," he told the Gunner in precise tones. "You are honored guest of the Reevers."

Whaleman met the fierce gaze and nodded his head in understanding. He had, of course, been thoroughly indoctrinated regarding the pathetic Reevers. They were like children—emotional, undisciplined, unstable. He could humor them for awhile.

"I have three days," he replied stiffly. "Then I must return to Terra 10. It is vital."

"You'll return all right," Tom Cole assured him, smiling. "Even a Reever understands the importance of Terra 10." Then he laughed softly and moved toward the hatch as the gravcar touched down.

Whaleman did not feel particularly reassured. He glanced out the viewport and sighed with resignation. The Reevers outside were behaving like lunatics, dancing about, turning cartwheels, slapping hands together and chanting an emotional cry of blurred words. Except for infrequent visits to Board Island, this was the Gunner's first adult touchdown on the mother planet. He had been down once, as a child of five, just prior to his matriculation at the Defense Academy at Moonport. Even so, he wished he had gone with the Homan GovTech who had offered him her bed and body for the night. Homan sex or not, it would have been preferable to spending his first adult holiday on earth in an insane asylum.

Whaleman steeled himself as he stepped through the hatch and into the tumultuous reception. *How tragic*, he thought. *How terribly, terribly tragic.*

It seemed that he was being welcomed as some sort of visiting deity. As a matter of fact, he was. He represented, to the Reevers, the final desperate gamble for man in a world of machines. But none, except perhaps Tom Cole, were even dimly aware of the staggering obstacles that lay asprawl that gamble.

Cole clasped the tall Gunner to him in a rough embrace and rumbled, "Welcome home, Zach Whaleman."

"Home?" Whaleman echoed weakly, his eyes on a reception line of cavorting Reevers.

The Reever chief nodded solemnly, replying, "Yes, the *only* home for man in the universe. You *are* a man, aren't you, Zach Whaleman?"

Numbly, the Gunner of Terra 10 moved into the dancing throng without replying. *Of course*, he thought, *I am a man. But what are these?*

CHAPTER TWO

An Impossible Dream

Several hours prior to his kidnapping by the Tom Cole Raiders, Zach Whaleman had starred in an event which all of Solana uneasily awaited since the first faint evidence of alien life had been detected in the galactic corridor. For a world long free of aggressive violence, the problem of solar system defense was not an easy one to face. The Terra class solar-orbiting gunships had been conceived one hundred years earlier. Nine generations of the deepspace super-dreadnaughts had died in the design-computers. Construction of the tenth generation had actually been underway for two decades. After a seemingly interminable succession of glitches, redesigns, and modifications, Terra 10 had become a reality. A gleaming tifusion sphere, one-half mile in diameter whose primary batteries could annihilate sizeable planets, she was fully automated, practically self-maintaining, and absolutely impervious to any known force of man or nature. But she had been a long time a'coming.

Gunner Zach Whaleman was literally born to the problem, having been genetically programmed at conception for his future role as a Defense Command technologist-tactician. All twenty-five years of his lifetime had been focussed upon the event which was about to take place—the Demonstration/Readiness Exercises for the most awesome weapons system to emerge from man's technology. Fittingly, the exercises were being staged from the center of government and being televised throughout Solana.

The young Gunner, clad immaculately in the sky-blue tunic and space-black tights of the Defense Command, showed no hint of nervousness or discomfort as he faced the assembled corporate heads of Solana. Zach Whaleman's genes had not been engineered for nervousness. Also, no living being knew Terra 10 as Zach knew her. They had grown up together.

The twelve Directors of the Solan Corporation, the President, and the sixteen Vice-Presidents occupied positions on a crescent-shaped dais behind the Gunnery Console. The seat provided for the Chairman of the Board was vacant. A tradition, older than living memory, precluded public appearances by the corporation's highest officer. Above and behind the dais, the chamber was filled with lesser administrative officers from the satellite communities.

Automated televisors hovered inconspicuously overhead to relay the scene to viewers around the solar system. Whaleman was very much aware that at the moment he was being watched by perhaps ninety-nine per cent of the human race. He bowed in an almost imperceptible movement of the waist and introduced himself in the precise monotones which were characteristic of Defense Commanders.

"Gunner Zachary Whaleman, Technical Commander, Solana's Gunship Terra 10," he announced. He paused briefly and then continued in the same clipped delivery. "First firing exercise is Secondary Battery of Anti-Gravity Diffusioneers. Short term, AGRAD. Range is zero to 3,000 nautmiles. Target will traverse gunnery envelope at 2.87 thousand nautmiles. Second firing is Primary Battery of Matter/Anti-Matter Emitters. Short term, MAME. Range is 2,000 to .9 million nautmiles. Target will enter gunnery envelope at .85 million."

The tall Gunner, a splendid specimen of disciplined masculinity six and a half feet high, moved smoothly to the console and eased into the command chair.

The Gunnery Console, specially installed for the exercises, was a duplicate of the regular controller at Moonbase. A large viewscreen at the upper left showed various exterior views of the gunship as she idled in a thousand-mile parking orbit of the earth. An adjacent screen provided the target display, and could accommodate simultaneously a target for each of Terra 10's forty guns.

Whaleman activated a control circuit and immediately a target drone appeared in the right-hand display. So perfect was the picture that even the markings on the 40-foot cylinder could be read. The other screen showed Terra 10 from eight views as she performed an automatic four-degree axis roll and slipped about to an eight-degree polar declination. A twelve-foot diameter gunport slid open, and the focal grid of an AGRAD battery began its pulsing dance.

For the benefit of the viewers, Whaleman explained: "AGRAD target acquisition is automatic. Gross adjustment is to nearest appropriate gun." He pointed out an indicator on the console. "Target Scan now makes fine adjustment."

An amber light began pulsing in the upper right quadrant of the deep space scanner, and simultaneously the drone on the target screen became outlined in a well defined halo.

Immediately, a robot voice from the unmanned gunship came through a speaker in the console: "Terra 10 reports target acquisition, AGRAD Six."

The Gunner nudged a communicator control with his knee and replied, "Confirmed, acquisition positive, target positive. Maintain." He turned in half-profile to the audience and explained, "At present, all firings are initiated by Moonbase. Eventually Terra 10 will be programmed to fire

automatically at any valid target intruding upon
her defense envelope. We demonstrate now a
Moonbase clearance and a Terra 10 automatic
firing sequence."

Whaleman returned his attention to the console. His fingers danced across a line of staggered
buttons, setting up the automatic firing mechanism. A *Path Control Positive* light began flashing
from the console. He threw the *Attack-Track* onto
"AGRAD Auto" and pulled the *Time Positive Line*
over beneath Battery Six.

"AGRAD Six on Automatic Ready," came the
robot report from the gunship.

"Terra 10 cleared to attack," Whaleman clipped back, his speech not much different than the
robot's.

The FIRE button immediately illuminated on
the Gunnery Console. The amber pulser of the
deep space scanner immediately became a steady
light, growing in brilliance and rapidly changing
color to a light pink and on through the shades of
red until it flared out and disappeared from the
electronic display. At that exact instant, the target
drone disappeared from the target screen.

"Target diffused," the robot announced.

"Confirmed," Whaleman responded. "Recycle
AGRAD Six to Standby. Secure from Automatic
Ready."

A murmur of voices was rising behind Whaleman. One official exclaimed, "Instant annihilation!
And at three thousand miles!"

Another gloated, "Wait until you see the
MAMEs in action. You'll dare anyone in the
universe to attack us!"

His face an emotionless mask, Whaleman was
busily setting up the next exercise. Inwardly, he
was elated over the reactions of his audience. A
long-awaited, impossible dream had become a

reality, and Gunner Whaleman had figured prominently in that transition. Even with nerveless genes, he had ample cause for elation.

A thousand miles from Board Island, scene of the demonstration, a somewhat different audience, at an agricultural station on the North American continent, exhibited a reaction that would have been found entirely disconcerting by Gunner Whaleman.

"That's our answer," declared Tom Cole, the self-proclaimed King of the Reevers. "We've got to get that gunship."

George (Hedge) Hedges/Bolsom, a six-footer with blond hair and pale skin, tore his Reever-blue eyes away from the televiewer long enough to acknowledge his chief's remark.

"How the corporation are we going to get that gunship, Tom?" he growled. "She's a thousand miles high right now and bound for Jupiter in just a few days."

The Reever leader had broodingly watched the cycling of the MAME batteries, as televised from Board Island.

We get the Gunner, Hedge," he replied tensely. "He's the key to the whole problem." He turned to the squatly powerful man at his other side, John (Blue) Fontainbleu Oraskny, a homan-sized four-and-a-half footer. "Blue, you run get Stel. And do it Mars quick. I want her to get a good look at that uniform."

Blue had been unhappy at the necessity for leaving the televiewer, but he hurried away toward the line of plastic domehuts flanking the clearing. All the men of the Reever commune, about eighty in number, were present to view the long-awaited exercises of Terra 10. The Reevers, bound forever to the garden planet by unchallengeable law, never missed a teleview of space events. They had gathered at the viewer in quiet bunches, all dressed identically in the prescribed transparent vests and black crotchguards, watching the proceedings with solemn interest. A soft murmur went up as Zach Whaleman punched the button on a MAME battery to explode a ten mile diameter meteoroid which was streaking through space nearly a million miles from Earth.

"By Mars, that's some shooting," Tom Cole had softly observed.

"I think this guy's a Reever, Tom," Hedge commented.

Cole chuckled. "What guy? The Gunner? Just because he's big and has red hair?"

"I never saw a normer look like that," Hedge insisted.

"Defense Commanders are different items," the Reever leader explained. "They're GPC'd for that extra size." He laughed. "Bet your appleseeds, Hedge, the screens gave that boy a *thorough* shakedown before he ever put that uniform on."

Whaleman was recycling the MAME batteries when Blue returned with a tall golden-haired beauty in tow. The girl wore nothing but a crotchguard. Heavy but shapely breasts jiggled in free suspension as she crossed over to Cole and Hedge. Tom Cole gave her a welcoming smile and pointed to the televiewer.

"Get a good look at him," he commanded.

The girl turned interested eyes to the screen. "He's beautiful," she murmured. "Who is it?"

"Terra 10's Gunner," Cole replied. "Think your women can whip up some outfits like that one?"

She frowned thoughtfully, concentrating on the Defense Command uniform. "It's not plastic."

Hedge snorted, "Bet your bubbling beauties it's not!"

"We might have some synfab that's close enough," the girl said. "But I don't know about the insignia." She nervously pinched a softly flaring hip and added, "I believe we can come up with something passable."

"Then do it," Cole snapped. "For me, and for all of Team One. You have our sizes."

The girl nodded. "How soon?"

"Two hours."

She rapidly blinked her eyes, then said, "All right. Two hours." Her eyes flashed a final appraisal toward the televiewer. "So that's a Gunner," she said softly, and quickly moved away.

Hedge watched the girl's swaying departure and asked, "What's the plan, Tom?"

"I been thinking about it ever since they announced these exercises. I guess we got to go to Board Island."

Hedge and Blue exchanged nervous glances. Hedge said, "Uh-huh. How the corporation we going to get there, Tom?"

"We'll ride the Board's commissary shuttle."

Blue rubbed his forehead and stared stonily at the ground. "That means we have to tackle Boob," he muttered.

Tom Cole nodded and absently rubbed his own head. "Makes me hurt just to think about it, but that's what we got to do."

Irritably, Hedge said, "I thought you was working something to neutralize that monster."

"I am," Cole replied. "But it's not ready yet. And Terra 10 is. So . . . " He turned slowly and gazed toward the distribution center, barely visible above the treetops.

"So we go without the neutralizer," Hedge said unhappily.

"That's the idea," Cole muttered. "Blue, you spread the word. I want volunteers. We got to get

Team One aboard that shuttle. That means a
diversion team. I need about twenty men to draw
Boob away long enough for us to get aboard." He
peered into the sky, frowned, and added, "Sun's
going down. It'll be dark by the time Stel gets
those uniforms ready. Mars! I wish that just once
we could have the odds on our side!"

"We got the odds, Tom," Blue assured his
leader, grinning. "We got *you*." He lightly punched
Cole on the arm and moved into a group of young
men who were still entranced by the distant
performance of the guns of Terra 10. "Hey!" he
cried urgently. "Tom's going to steal Terra 10! We
need some Boob bait."

Seconds later, the exciting news had flashed
throughout the small commune of Reevers. Tom
Cole was going to steal Terra 10! And the first
frame of another impossible dream was falling into
focus.

CHAPTER THREE

The Break-out

Tom Cole, or Tom Coleman/Seville as he was identified on official records, was a born revolutionary. Just as Zach Whaleman had been genetically engineered for his life role as a corporation gunner, Tom Cole's GPC code had been directed to a specific function—he was to have become a corporate manager or, at least, a government technician. Something in Tom's genetic structure had stubbornly resisted this programmed tampering, however, and shortly after his birth it was already evident that the infant was doomed to classification within that small percentage of GPC failures. He was an evolutionary revert, or "reever," with anomalies of both mind and body.

Many generations earlier, the human race had become optimized and homogenized into a "truly democratic" society wherein all members were equal in terms of size, color, intelligence, and emotional stability. *Homan* was the identifying term for these optimated humans who comprised roughly ninety-five percent of the Solan population, a pygmy race of ninety-pound physical weaklings, 4.5 feet tall, characteristically thin, tan-skinned, brown-haired, and brown-eyed. Only Defense Command candidates and a few additional rigorous-vocation groups escaped the optimization program. Homans generally regarded these exceptions as physical freaks—which indeed they were, in a world of 95% conformity—and as just a cut above the pathetic Reevers. The Reevers were themselves commonly regarded as mental incompetents and emotional misfits who could not be entrusted with the rights and privileges of a free society.

Tom Cole was a prime example of this latter contention. Conceived in a genetic revolt and born to a world long rid of "id" syndromes, it must have been inevitable that the fierce and independent nature of this "evolutionary throwback" would involve him in constant conflict with his social environment. He had been systematically moved from one Terran commune to another, finally reaching rock bottom in the tiny "maximum-dependency" village at AgSta 23, near the North American strip city of Yorkport.

AS-23 was a fruit station, producing nearly 10% of Solana's apples and pears. The sole responsibility of the Reevers there lay in the minimal human requirements of orchard maintenance. A small contingent of Homans, appropriately housed in a different sector of the orchards, saw to the technical requirements of harvesting, processing, packing, and shipping the bountiful yield at the station.

The Reevers were free to roam the orchards at will. They established their own working routines, and generally governed themselves. There were no fences and no human guards, but forbidden areas were patrolled by automated sentinels which the Reevers called "Boob" and which dealt out severe punishment to Reever trespassers.

Tom Cole's mind had been busy with the Boob problem on that evening of the Terra 10 exercises as he led his thirty-man party into the heart of AS-23, the distribution center. The ground complex of food processing and storage buildings occupied a grudging five acres of precious terran soil and rose 100 feet to a pentagonal arrangement of loading docks. The fully automated 24-hour facility had no requirement for artificial lighting, so there was none. The raiders crowded into the open at the edge of the clearing and stared mutely at the cluster of buildings silhouetted against the night sky. The dark bulk of an Ag Train of twenty linked vans hovered at the pentagon as loading automats busily transferred bulk fruits into the commodious holds.

Tom Cole balanced his seven-foot, 300-pound frame on the balls of his feet, stretched to his toes, sighed, and squeezed his forehead in a nervous gesture. "They're loading the Mercury supplier," he observed.

"Wonder where Boob is?" Blue commented, licking his lips.

"At the ground docks, no doubt," Cole replied. "He's always over there when the Board shuttle is looting the goodies."

He craned about to inspect his party. Ten, including Cole and Hedge, wore the blue and black uniforms of the Defense Command. The other twenty, the diversion teams were clad only in crotchguards and footskeins.

Blue was in charge of the diversion teams. He said, "Well, I guess there's only one way to find out for sure. I'll send—"

"No, wait!" Cole interrupted. "We'll leave you here. Give us time to get over there opposite the ground docks, then start your play. Once you're sure you have Boob's attention, *keep* it for a full minute. Better make it a minute and a half, if that's not stretching it too far. By that time, Team One will be snugly buttoned up inside the shuttle and you can break off. Tell your boys to be quick'n nimble and to play that fifty-yard line for all they're worth."

Blue nodded his understanding. "Shouldn't I send a few baiters over with you, just in case?"

"In case, what?"

"In case it takes him less'n a minute to get us all."

"In that case, buddy, just forget it," Cole told his lieutenant. "If you can't hold him, we can just forget the whole thing and go back to pruning apple trees the rest of our lives. You got to hold him, Blue."

"Okay," the squat little Reever replied. "We'll hold."

"Play it right, and there's no need for any of you getting hit. Just watch that fifty-yard line."

Blue sniffed. "That line can disappear mighty quick, Tom, when that beetle's riled."

"You just got to be quicker," Cole replied gruffly. He slapped Blue lightly on the cheek and mussed his hair, then grinned and waved Team One into the moonlit clearing. "Keep close to the trees, now," he commanded in a loud whisper. "And remember, Boob's got ears, too, so keep it quiet. Hedge, what're you doing? Keep 'em in a single file, eh."

The six-footer had been peering intently toward the shadows of the buildings, less than a hundred yards distant. "When Boob gets you once, you don't forget so easy," he said, smiling ruefully. "My head hurts just thinking about it."

"Mine, too," Blue murmured, following along with his departing comrades for a few yards. "All I can say is—make it worth while, eh? When we get those guns, the first thing I'm going to do is blast me a couple of Boobs."

Tom Cole's teeth gleamed momentarily as he turned back for a farewell wave, then he and the Boarders were out of sight in the shadows. Blue transferred his attention to the ominous hulk of activity directly ahead. Only the mechanical whirrings of the automats broke the night stillness.

Blue hunched his powerful shoulders in an involuntary shiver and began silently counting off the seconds. His baiters were taking up their practiced positions and getting ready for the rush. Blue was proud of them—plenty proud. Every one of them had been zingoed at least once by Boob—they all knew what awaited them out there. But they were men—*men*—not machines. Not homogenes. Not human caricatures. *Men*. And they were going out there to do a man's job.

Blue had set the offense as five four-man teams. One team would get out there and attract Boob's attention. That was the most dangerous phase because you never knew where the monster would strike from. Sometimes the first hint of his presence came with that ultrasonic wave blasting into the brain and jerking you around like a rag doll. After that, you didn't know much of anything, for days sometimes, except for the unrelenting pain and nausea.

A hundred and twenty seconds had passed since he began the count. Blue moved quietly out to the kickoff team and said, "Okay, get ready."

Fear gazed back at him from all four faces—but determination, also.

"We're ready," muttered a pink-cheeked youth.

Blue held his breath for a moment, his eyes straining into the shadows of the buildings, then commanded, "Go!"

Two of the baiters leapt off into a running penetration of the forbidden area, splitting off into a Y several yards out and pursuing diverging courses. As soon as the first two reached the midway point, the other two streaked out in an identical pattern. Blue held his arm high, waiting the proper moment to signal the next team's jump-off.

At the other side of the complex, Tom Cole and the boarding team waited in tense alertness some seventy yards clear of the ground level docks.

The Board Island commissary shuttle, a rather smallish van-type dense-atmosphere craft, occupied a loading stall in the packaged foods area. Directly opposite the shuttle stood the dreaded and ever-alert autosentinel, Boob.

Like a huge bug, complete with twitching antennae and unblinking eyes, it stood fifteen feet high on six deceptively fragile looking legs. The roundish body measured ten by fifteen feet and bristled with six ultrasonic guns which could fire simultaneously at six different targets. Boob fired first and never asked questions, attacking one and all of the human race who ventured into the fifty-yard range of his gun-sensors. Somehow, though, and Tom Cole was still trying to understand it, only Reevers were affected by those ultrasonic blasts from the Boob guns. The Homan technicians could walk calmly about their duties in a veritable flood of Boob waves, while even a near-miss was enough to scramble a Reever's brains for hours.

Hedge whispered, "Tom, I don't think—" then stopped talking abruptly, frozen by a sudden movement of the autosentinel.

"Huh, he's smelling the bait," Cole grunted.

The sentry's antennae had begun to lash about, the eyes glowing with a reddish light, and it was shifting in a sideways movement. Cole smiled grimly as the distant cries of "Hey, Boob!" floated across the clearing. The autosentinel moved with incredible speed then, the six legs meshing into furious motion as the ugly machine disappeared into the darkness between the buildings.

"That's it—let's go!" Cole commanded in a harsh whisper. He flung himself into the open and sprinted for the commissary van, his long legs rapidly closing the gap and the others jumping off at ten yard intervals and single-filing behind him in a disciplined rush toward dignity, and freedom, and manhood.

Blue heard his kickoff men sounding the "Hey, Boob!" baiting cry and immediately brought his arm down in a swift chop to send the stunting team into no-man's-land. They looped off in a loose X-formation, echoing the baiting cry as they ran. A scream came from the darkness in the kickoff team's area, and Blue knew then that contact had been established.

"Contact!" he yelled, and led the trap teams into a carefully planned maneuver designed to bedevil and frustrate the Solan Corporation's last and only word on Reever-containment.

The final eight men of the boob-bait detail advanced cautiously, in a precise semi-circle, spaced at ten-yard intervals. Another scream from the shadowed area near the buildings further pinpointed the autosentinel's location. Two panting members of the kickoff team hove into view.

As Blue signaled them into the semi-circle, one gasped, "The stunters are bringing 'im over!"

"Tom needs another minute," Blue growled, continuing the precision advance. An instant later, Boob crabbed into the moonlight, antennae whipping menacingly, the big crystal eyes blazing in circular sweeps.

Two stunt men raced in against his right flank. An antenna quivered, curled, then froze momentarily as a sensor took the reading. The stunters dug in, reversed, and crossed each other in a diving leap. An ultrasonic gun whirred, missed, and corrected as one of the stunters, a wiry youth with flying hair, realized that he had crossed the invisible safety line and frantically flipped into a rolling tumble toward the outside. The gun whirred again. The youth screamed and leapt into air as a

sudden electrical storm erupted in his brain and
convulsed the entire neuromuscular structure. He
crashed to the ground and writhed about in an
epileptic-like seizure. His partner shouted, "Hey
Boob!" and ran a tight figure-eight pattern directly
in front of the blazing eyes. Meanwhile, Blue's
harassment circle had been forged, and Boob was
surrounded by taunting, dancing, and stunting
Reevers. They had learned their lessons well, and
were executing with precision.

The Boob guns were whirring ceaselessly, now,
as the big machine crabbed and plunged, knelt and
leapt, fired and missed and fired again and again at
the fast-moving profusion of targets. Here and
there, a man would scream and twitch to the
ground in mindless spasm.

Blue, standing calmly at the edge of the
fire-zone, was picking up fringe-area reverbs of the
zinging ultrasonic blasts but stubbornly held his
ground, both hands to his head, barking the signals
of play. Half of his force now lay shuddering and
twitching on the ground. Still, the autosentinel was
being held prisoner of his own sensors as it blindly
reacted to each parry of the Reevers, shuttling
back and forth, wheeling in erratic circles and
firing at every movement across its perceptor
zones.

Blue reached the minute-and-a-half count when
he fell to his knees and vomited. Through the
retching, he yelled, "Break—break and run!" and
flung himself into a wild roll toward the trees.

The command came a split second too late.
The Boob's sense-computer had already resolved
the crosstug effect of the Reevers' attack. One
sensory bank abruptly went dead and the monstrous automat made a lunge in the other direction,
immediately stunning the three men on its live
side.

Before the others could react to the sudden offensive tactic, the Boob's sensors had cycled to the other side. Blue was struck less than ten yards from the trees, and curled into a shuddering fetal ball. The remainder of the Reevers fell quickly.

The bug's readers were immediately cognizant of the rapidly lowering life-signs in the battle area. The antennae quivered and jerked in the direction of the ground level docks, and Boob scuttled smoothly and silently across the open ground toward the pulse of pounding hearts.

Tom Cole, leaning far out of the open hatch of the Board Island shuttle, dragged the tenth man inside just as the autosentinel reappeared. He pushed the man to the floor, whispered, "Quiet now, quiet," and made his way cautiously to the viewport as the big bug swung angrily around the dock area. "Hold your breath," he quietly advised his team. "Slow your heartbeat all you can. Get relaxed, be a vegetable, don't move, don't make a sound."

Boob made two complete passes around the shuttle, antennae waving in a furious search, then halted, wheeled slowly about, scuttled over to its earlier sentry station, folded in its legs, and settled quietly to the ground.

"Good," Cole whispered. "He's recharging. Everybody stay put and think sweet thoughts."

One man was forced to move several minutes later to make way for the loading automat. He did so slowly and quietly.

After another ten minutes of tense stillness, the loader departed and the hatch slid shut. Seconds later, the automated craft rose vertically from the dock and slipped into the departure corridor, circling slowly over the clearing. Hedge moved up beside Tom Cole at the viewport.

"Close," Hedge said quietly. "Too damn close."

"Yeah," Cole replied. "But look at that down there." The shuttle was passing directly over the site of the Boob-baiting. "Looks like he zingoed all of 'em."

"There's Blue over by the apples," Hedge muttered. "Damn, Tom. Those are mighty fine boys. They deserve a medal."

The anti-gravity shuttle had reached the release point and was now accelerating in a smooth climb for altitude. Tom Cole watched the moonswept terrain as it rapidly receded. He sighed, turned to Hedge, and smiled.

"I'm going to give them the guns of Terra 10, Hedge," he said softly, then turned from the viewport with a smile and added, "and then I'm going to give them Mother Earth."

"Think you can really do that, Tom?" Hedge muttered.

"Did you think we'd really break out of 23?" Cole countered.

Hedge grinned. "We did, didn't we."

"Bet your appleseeds," Cole said. "Better still, throw 'em away. But not yet—not yet. The whole thing hinges on us getting that Gunner. Somehow, we've got to get that Gunner."

And, of course, they got that Gunner.

CHAPTER FOUR

Trembling Genes

Zach Whaleman's GPC height potential had been engineered for 6.5 feet, skeletal scale medium-heavy. These physical attributes, typical of the elite Defense Commanders, had been attained by his fifteenth year of growth, and would alone have been enough to insure his notability in any human crowd. Add to this the anomaly of flaming red hair and startlingly blue eyes, and Zach Whaleman was physically more at home with the Reevers than with any other segment of the human race. However, any hint or suggestion that Whaleman may have been born with a reversion of critical genes had been systematically analyzed and rejected early in his life.

A seventh generation conception of the same genetic pattern, the infant Whaleman moreover had been officially graded as "superior" material for the Defense Command Academy. The anomalies were apparently confined to hair and eyes. All other results of the preconception engineering had been right on mark. His physical reference was perfect. He was mentally brilliant with a high aptitude for advanced technology. He would be a natural "loner," inclined toward selfless service, introverted toward an inner strength and drive for self-realization. He would be resolute and self-reliant. These qualities made Whaleman a natural for the defense command, they also would render him a hopeless misfit in most human undertakings.

Those programmed for satellite-community work, for example, depended almost exclusively upon communal type team living for their greater satisfactions in life. Mining and materials technicians, on the other hand, while personalized in the direction of self-sufficiency in a manner similar to the Defense Commanders, had been found to be more efficient when imbued with an egoistic flair for discovery of self via the accolades received after a discovery of new materials or processes. Government technicians, possessing the same Whaleman genes for selfless service, found their most effective modification in an impersonal drive toward universal justice and goodwill, with a strong brake on self-reliance and too much independent action.

Zach Whaleman, and his "superior" genes, had sailed through the usual social indoctrination phase during his third and fourth years of life. Matriculating at the Defense Academy in his fifth year, he was graduated with honors at the age of twenty, was awarded the rank of Gunner, and immediately assigned to postgraduate work at Mercury Four where Terra 10 was going through final outfitting.

For five years, Whaleman lived aboard the big gunship, overseeing the installation of her batteries and other operational systems, becoming familiar with her power plants and support systems, and working out various engineering modifications.

At the brief commissioning ceremony at Mercury Four, he had been presented with the formal letter of TechCom (Technical Commander), denoting his personal responsibility for the awesome weapons system. Terra 10 was his. He would not, as a rule, live aboard the big ship. She had been designed for robot-remote operation, and Whaleman's sojourns aboard the gleaming sphere would be limited to infrequent maintenance and modification calls. He would, though, ride her into the initial solar orbit, perform final checkout and alignment routines, and prepare the space dreadnaught for her defense responsibilities in the solar-access corridor. This was the consideration uppermost in Whaleman's mind as he fretted through that first night at Ag-Sta 23. He would humor the Reevers to whatever extent allowed by his timetable if necessary, though, he would resort to stern measures in order to get back aboard Terra 10 in time to receive the ferry squadron.

Actually, Whaleman had talked himself into an acceptance of the situation. He had really formed no plans for filling that three-day time interval before the ferry squadron would be ready to engage Terra 10, and after the initial shock of being kidnapped had worn off, the Defense Commander was finding his enforced visit pleasant enough. The food was good, his quarters adequate, and the heavy atmosphere of the continent sweet with the natural perfumes of growing things.

Almost nostalgically he found himself standing at the open window and gazing up into the pre-dawn skies, thinking of that first visit, so long ago, to this jewel of the solar system, the garden planet Earth. He had been but five years old, a precocious candidate for the Defense Command, enjoying his final cohabitation leave with his parents, Defense Techs Paul Whaler and Joan Mannson. Whaleman remembered little of that first excursion to Earth—only a vague sensing of incredible landscape colorations and almost overpowering scents—and not much more of his parents. He pushed into the edges of the memories, deliberately so, and found not a five-year-old's remembrance of a strange planet but a little boy's time-diminished appreciation of those two strangers whom he had called Mother and Father.

Paul Whaler he remembered as towering, broad, and given to booming laughter. He particularly remembered that laugh. It had been a source of embarrassment to his mother. Paul had told him about the human race populating itself off of

Earth, and had taken him about in a sky sled to show Zach how the entire planet had been converted into a giant garden in order to provide food for the exploding and now exiled population of Solana—exiled from Earth, of course. There was no room left for people on the Mother Planet, Paul had explained. Every precious square inch of arable land, on this only life-producing planet in the known universe, was under cultivation, and even then the bulk of mankind's diet was synthesized.

Yes, Zach Whaleman remembered Paul Whaler, even though he had spent less than thirty days altogether with his father. And he remembered Joan Mannson. There had been periods, long ago, when he had dreamed of Joan Mannson nearly every night. She was tall, too, as he recalled, very beautiful, attentive to her stranger-son whenever they were together, forever fussing with Zach's flaming head of hair—as though, perhaps, she was a bit self-conscious or even embarrassed by the startling anomaly. He did not remember much else about his parents. He had not seen them or the continents of Earth since, and felt no particular sense of loss, except after an occasional dream of lying snuggled to Joan Mannson's chest, or upon hearing some veteran defense commander's tall tales of Mother Earth. Occasionally, as a child, he would stand there at the observation deck of the Academy and gaze out upon that glowing ball in the sky and try to remember the scents and vivid colors and wonder if he dreamed all that, also.

Even the dreams of Joan Mannson had become lost after his fourth year at the Academy, the evolution of a gunner being in full spiral and with little of extraneous interests to detract from that development.

At about that point in life when his vocal chords began playing tricks on him and his penis became an object of more than casual interest, Whaleman's berthing assignment was abruptly shuffled, and he found himself sharing a billet with Laney Furr-Roberts, a thirty-year-old female Education Tech who brought alive again the muted memories of Joan Mannson's chest.

The memories again fled, though, this time under the dedicated ministrations of the EdTech who taught him of life's little social rewards via a course labeled "*Erotic Indoctrination.*" One year later to the day, Zach's billeting was changed again, to a co-ed dorm, and he saw Laney Furr-Roberts no more except in infrequent and disturbing dreams which seemed to be a blurred composite of Laney and Joan Mannson.

The billets had changed with almost monotonous regularity after that, varying from co-ed, to privacy, to all-male, to robot-companion and then back to co-ed again, during which cycles Zach learned that the sex expression has many facets, none clearly superior to another.

At the age of eighteen, he was transferred to the isolation of intensive gunner training and taught to cope with an imposed asceticism. This, he quickly deduced, was the most difficult phase of his sexual training. He refused to use the chemical depressants offered, instead working out his own mental techniques for suppressing the natural hungers of vibrant youth. This pleased his examiners and added to the overall honors with which he was graduated two years later.

The five years on Terra 10 had, of course, been all but sublime. They represented, to Zach Whaleman, the realization of a lifelong goal. The human expression took a back seat, and the young gunner became almost indistinguishable from the robots alongside which he worked.

This interlude on Earth, under somewhat different circumstances, could have been downright pleasant for Whaleman—or so he was thinking as he stood at the open window of the Reever hut and watched that awe-inspiring miracle of Terran sunrise. And as the growing radiance split the gray shadows of dawn, Zach saw another awe-inspiring sight.

She stood nearly as tall as Whaleman, just outside his window, long yellow hair tumbling in heavy folds down her back—a golden giantess, nude except for a black triangle of shiny plastic at the base of her abdomen, regarding him with a level and unblinking gaze of luminous eyes, deepest blue, large, set into the lovely head at most commanding angles, wide-spaced, *strange*. Her flesh all over seemed to glow with an inner light—Zach supposed it was a trick of the Terran sunrise. Massive hips exploded outward from nipped waist and oval tummy.

Most interesting to Whaleman were the fantastic breastworks, huge swollen globes of shiny flesh upon her chest, crowned with soft pink suckler tips—no doubt, the Gunner surmised—the mammary evidence of a runaway GPC maternal code. He realized that he was inspecting her with excessive interest but could not help himself. The mammala were exquisitely formed, curiously hard-soft in appearance, and jutting out from the chest in a manner that aroused Whaleman's engineering curiosity.

He dragged his eyes away from the redshade-1 provocative tips and raised them to meet the girl's steady gaze. He felt curiously self-conscious and over-formal as he introduced himself.

"Gunner Zach Whaleman," he said with soft precision.

The girl acknowledged with a curt nod. "I know. I am Stel Rogers/Brandt."

The words came to Whaleman as a breathlessly musical blur. He said, "Request slow speak, unskronk."

She repeated the statement in a careful delivery, her facial expression unchanging. Whaleman nodded his understanding and returned once again to an inspection of her chest area. The Gunner had, of course, received elemental education in such anomalies, but this was the first breasted woman he had seen in the flesh. He reached through the window and carefully touched one of the interesting projections, then thoughtfully examined the suckler tip between thumb and finger. The girl stiffened slightly but allowed him to continue the examination, the hint of a smile forming at her lips.

"Mammala first view," he solemnly informed her, as though to explain his interest.

Her smile grew. She said, "Be kind to Reevers."

The Gunner's hand quickly dropped away. "Apology," he murmured. He touched his head, drawing attention to his own hair. "Anomaly," he pointed out. "Like same."

The girl laughed and reached out to run her fingers lightly across the Defense Command insignia on his tunic. A flowing stream of words were mixed in with the musical laughter. He cocked his head and concentrated on her swiftly moving lips, but received only gibberish. She read the dismay on his face and abruptly halted.

"Sorry," she said soberly. "I forgot. Slow speak. I was just telling you of the terrible time I had duplicating that insignia. Yours is a threaded fabric. I had to use synfab, and the darned stuff splits, and runs and just doesn't cooperate at all."

Whaleman caught the words that time, but together they meant nothing at all, and the non-communication disturbed him. The animation

of the girl's face disturbed him. The swollen
suspensions at her chest disturbed him. Her height
and otherwise angular litheness he found entirely
pleasing and comparable to the Defense Command
females of his own natural environment. But those
mammaries! And that *speech!* ·

He forced a smile and said, "You think in
language. I do not. Regrets, we do not communicate—regrets."

He swung away from the window, dismissing
the girl and expecting her to go away.

She did not go away. She went around to the
door and entered the hut, eyed the interior, and
said, "You did not sleep."

"I will sleep to Jupiter," he curtly replied, as
though speaking to a disfavored child. "Skronk?"

"No," the girl replied, moving directly in front
of him. "I do not skronk, machine man."

"I am human," Whaleman said.

"Humans sleep every night," she informed him.

"Reevers, maybe. Homans, yes." The Gunner
smiled. "Not Commanders. Sleep cycle, three-day.
Skronk? Conscious cycle, ten-day. Skronk?"

The girl was frowning. "I heard that," she said
quietly. "I did not believe it. It is *true* then? You
can go for ten whole days without sleeping?"

The Gunner solemnly nodded his head. "Is
more efficient. In deepspace, night is day and day
is night, is like same."

The girl had moved very close to him. The
nearness unaccountably bothered him. He pushed a
hand into the long golden hair and thoughtfully
caressed it.

"Hair is beautiful—" he said, "but inefficient."

The girl's musical laughter filled the hut, the
heavy breasts swaying and jiggling in a most
disconcerting manner. The Gunner released the
golden hair and quickly back-stepped. A strange,
dreamlike feeling was enveloping him.

The laughter had conjured visions of Paul Whaler, the long forgotten stranger-father—and Whaleman found himself once again staring at the suckler tips of the mammaries and wondering what had become of Joan Mannson. He wondered if those fantastic mammala were as uncomfortable for the girl as they appeared to be, and he wondered what those sucklers would feel like between a baby's lips . . .

The long-exiled Terran was full of wonderment. In just a short while, he would be wondering about the tie that could bind across a thousand years of human evolution. At the moment, he was wondering about the incomprehensible magnetism which seemed to be drawing him compellingly to this simple Reever. Sexual attraction Whaleman could understand, but this present feeling went far beyond such elemental biologics.

The girl had taken his hand and was tugging him through the doorway. "Come on," she said, enunciating carefully, "I am going to show you something *terribly* inefficient. I want you to see our waterfall."

Whaleman was trying to visualize falling water. He presumed that the girl was offering him a bath. He found his lips twisting into the strangely broad smile of the Reevers, and decided that he could learn to like these simple people. "Yes," he said, going along unprotestingly, "water falling is good."

"Zach, you're a different item," she declared, giggling and squeezing his hand. She led him across the compound and into the orchard.

The almost overpowering aroma of apple blossoms filled his nostrils and intensified the strange tugging at his psyche. He halted suddenly to pluck a blossom from a low branch and rolled it between his fingers then raised it to his nose for a deeper smell.

As Stel watched him, a tender expression moved into her face. Zach flashed her an almost guilty look, then knelt suddenly to plunge his fingers into the soft soil of earth at the base of the tree. Shaking inwardly with a strangeness which he was beginning to identify as *emotion*, the Gunner rubbed the dirt into his palms, tasted it, hastily spat it out, and grinned self-consciously at his companion.

"Come on," she said, pulling at him with an almost pitying smile.

"Mother Earth," he said, rising hastily. "First close view. Womb of life, home of man."

Stel Rogers/Brandt was obviously affected by the display of embarrassed emotion. She said, "Yes," softly, and pulled him on to a small footbridge which spanned an irrigation canal.

They crossed over and swerved abruptly into a shallow ravine and began a gradual climb around the side of a hill. A growing roar in the air discouraged conversation, which neither seemed to be in the mood for, anyway. Their route brought them beside a rushing brook. The girl pulled Whaleman into the water, which was frigid and ankle-deep, and led him up the twisting bed of the rock-strewn stream.

The Gunner's feet were squishing in his soft footgear and beginning to ache with the cold. He wondered vaguely if he was expected to actually bathe in the frigid water, and then they took another sharp turn and came onto a wide rock ledge beneath the most awesome view of the Gunner's young life.

An endless torrent of crystal-clear water spilled down a 300-foot course in a nearly vertical fall, roaring with an unvarying intensity. Whaleman froze, unbreathing for a long moment, his head inclined in a rapturous gaze at the tumbling water, then he released his pent breath and a myriad of emotions played across his upturned face.

Stel moved her lips close to his ear to make herself heard above the roar of the falls and said, "Beautiful, isn't it?"

"Is more . . . *feeling*," Whaleman replied, groping for words beyond his reach.

"A religious feeling," Stel agreed.

Whaleman solemnly nodded his head and said, "Religious, yes. The feeling is religious."

They stood there for long minutes while the spaceman soaked up the "religious feeling," then Stel tugged him out of the stream and led him along a circular path to a small glade on the hillside. Sunlight was pouring through the trees and lighting the pastoral scene with a shimmering halo-like effect. Looking back toward the waterfall, she pointed out a rainbow hovering in the mist.

"I'll bet you've never viewed one of those," she told him.

"Mother planet has many beauties," Whaleman replied in awed tones.

Stel dropped to her knees, then toppled over to lie on her back, twisting to one side from the hips down. The Gunner stared at her, his eyes flicking rapidly from heaving bosom to upflung hip. "Yes, many beauties," he said.

She patted the soft turf invitingly. Whaleman knelt, gathered her in his arms, and kissed her, running a hand exploringly along the soft lines of the magnificently female body. She pushed his hand away and broke the kiss.

"Watch that," she said half-angrily. "I'm not a social robot."

The Gunner's face was reflecting confused emotions. "Companions," he said in a thickening voice. "You, me, sexual companions."

Stel shook her head and replied, "It does not work that way here." She pushed away from his embrace and rose to an elbow, staring steadily at the spaceman. "You have to be in love."

Whaleman made himself comfortable beside her, carefully studied her face, and presently said, "Unskronk."

"That's your trouble," she replied, sighing. "You don't skronk anything but machines."

"Skronk love," Whaleman argued. "Love Solana. Love Terra. Love all mankind. Even Reevers. Love Stel Rogers/Brandt."

"That isn't the kind of love I mean," the girl told him. She pointed to the waterfall. "You skronk the religious feeling?"

"Religious is feel different," he said.

"Sex love is feel different, too," Stel replied. "You have to love me like that, like religious feeling. *Then* maybe, we can be sex companions."

Whaleman's eyes were traveling slowly. "Skronk, like Joan Mannson."

"Who is Joan Mannson?"

"Joan Mannson is female parent. My mother." He had never before audibly referred to Joan Mannson using that specific term. His voice was noticeably lower as he added, "Is religious like feeling love."

Stel said hesitantly, "No, not exactly."

The Gunner firmly nodded his head. "Is like Joan Mannson feeling. Plus sex feeling." He tenderly fondled her breast and leaned over to gently kiss the swell.

The girl sucked in her breath, curled her fingers into a shock of red hair, and tugged his head clear. "You're not going to seduce me, Zach," she said firmly. "You have to understand. You have to love me like—like . . . "

Whaleman pushed her flat and nuzzled her throat, then drew back to gaze soberly into her eyes. "This is difference," he said solemnly. "First view, Reevers. First view, Stel Rogers/Brandt. First view, Mother Earth. Religious, yes. Like waterfall. Like Joan Mannson and Laney Furr-Roberts combined. Yes. Same, like dreaming, like strangeness inside."

"Gosh that's beautiful, Zach," Stel whispered.

"Yes, also beautiful. Zach loves Stel Rogers/Brandt like religious waterfall. Like Joan Mannson plus sex. Not like indoctrinator. Not like co-ed. Not like robot companion. Zach loves Stel like Terra, like orchards, like soil, like waterfall. Plus sex."

The girl draped a hand across her eyes and, forgetting to "slow speak," murmured, "You big robot, go on back to your moon and your machines. They're going to grind you up down here."

The words came to Whaleman as an emotional blur. He understood only that he had somehow saddened her. Already he had begun to alter his opinion of the Reever mind. There was more there, he realized now, than a casual contact would reveal. He felt vaguely ashamed of himself without even understanding the cause of his discomfort. He raised to his knees, the bafflement showing plainly in his eyes. With laboring difficulty, he presented a halting apology.

"Unskronk Terra. Unskronk Reevers. Apology, apology, unskronk Reever sex."

Stel uncovered her eyes. They were moist, adding to the Gunner's discomfort. She said slowly, "Zach, you're not really human—you know that. You might be a lord of the heavens, but you're a helpless babe down here in these woods. Contrary to what you have been taught, Reevers are not idiots. Certainly not Tom Cole, and he—"

Whaleman interrupted with, "I am human. Not robot. Social speak is difficult . . . language is . . . not usual—skronk? I learn speak social for Stel, we skronk together—each other."

"I just want you to understand what you're up against," she declared hotly. "That's all. You're dealing with human beings here, not machines, not homans, but the absolute cream of humanity."

"Unskronk," Whaleman replied, smiling.

"Things are not like you think they are," she persisted. "Know thy enemy! The Reevers are not emotional children. Try to understand that!"

The Gunner was thinking about it. He smiled suddenly and said, "Stel *is* emotional child. This is difference. This is religious feeling."

She scrambled to her feet. "Just remember, later, that I warned you!"

Whaleman was grinning, understanding only that she was no longer saddened.

"Companions later," he said, "post-skronk. You help me think social. I help you skronk beauties." He waved his hand in a circle of the heavens. " . . . out there. Where man is, beauty is, even deepspace."

"You don't understand a thing I've told you," she said.

"We have two days," Whaleman told her. "Then I return to Terra 10."

"That's what I'm telling you," Stel replied dismally. "When you return to Terra 10, you'll be going back with a full escort."

"Escort, yes. Ferry squadron, deepspace cruisers, tow gunship to Jovian envelope."

"I'm not talking about the ferry squadron. I mean the Reevers."

Whaleman gave her a blank look. "Reevers cannot leave Terra."

"That's what *you* think."

"Unskronk," Whaleman replied with a troubled frown.

"You'd better start skronking," Stel said. "Tom Cole wants Terra 10, and if you don't help him, he'll grind you—"

"Slow speak," Whaleman interrupted, grinning.

"There's not a thing you can do to stop it," the girl replied, carefully enunciating, "but I want you to know what to expect. Tom Cole is going to steal Terra 10, and you're going to help him—alive or dead. Do you skronk that? Alive or dead!"

Whaleman stared at her through a moment of thoughtful silence. Then he began to laugh, the sounds booming out in musical claps, and deep in his mind was an overlapping vision of Paul Whaler, also laughing, and a shadowy picture of Tom Cole seated at the control console of Terra 10. It was, for Whaleman, the first genuine laughter of a quiet lifetime.

"What's so funny?" the girl asked, frowning.

"Yes, funny, this is funny," the Gunner replied, dabbing with surprise at the moisture rolling down his cheeks. "Is funny, Tom Cole in Terra 10. This is funny, funny!"

"Watch it," Stel said coolly. "You could die laughing."

CHAPTER FIVE

A Genetic Difference

Over the centuries, genetic engineering had developed into a very precise science. Long before Zach Whaleman's birth, the Solan Corporation's medical administrators had become satisfied that all goals of the Genetically Programmed Conception plan had been fully met. The small percentage of failures, personified by the Reevers, was regarded as an unavoidable incidence and statistically unimportant. There were, after all, less than ten thousand living Reevers in a total Solan population of 17.3 billion.

A minority report, early in the program, had expressed fears that many more latent Reevers were enjoying the free society of Solana but no evidence had ever been presented to back up this assumption. As for the successes, these spoke for themselves. Crime no longer existed among the normal population. Gone, also, was aggressiveness except in specific and carefully directed areas of human activity. Practically all of the troubling and destructive aspects of mankind had been eliminated—greed, avarice, hatreds—all were relics of the past.

Zach Whaleman, during that first day of his enforced visit at AS 23, was beginning to realize something of the full price which the human race had paid for these "advances."

One day with the Reevers was enough to produce troubling questions in the young Gunner's mind, questions which were forcibly brought into the light of open discussion by his host.

"For generations beyond counting," Tom Cole told Whaleman that first evening, "the corporation has been systematically dehumanizing the human race. What they call 'progress' is actually a programmed extinction of everything human."

Gunner Whaleman did not wish to be disagreeable, nor did he wish to be cast into the unenviable position of debating matters of high policy with an unevolved member of his race. He was learning, moreover, that the Reever mind had been vastly underrated—at least, in his own thinking—and he was interested in determining the extent of Reever logic. He carefully pondered Coleman/Seville's statement and formulated a non-argumentative reply.

"This could be true," he said soberly. "Emphasis for evolution has been eradication of animal behavior. Goal is toward more man, less savage. Reason, not emotion. Dedication, not greed. Love, not hate."

They were seated on plastic bubblechairs in the commune pavilion. A dozen or so couples were dancing in the moonlight to canned music. Stel Rogers/Brandt and a non-breasted beauty who was introduced as Sofia Scala/Lowen completed the foursome at the chieftain's table. Sofia looked like any normal woman except for long black hair and extremely flared hips. Also, she wore apple blossoms in her hair. Whaleman thought the latter adornment extremely charming.

"There's the rub," Tom Cole said to Whaleman. "What happens to love when you've killed all the emotions? When you bland all the emotion out of love, what is left? Mars, an automat can be dedicated and loyal."

"Why are they talking like machines?" the dark-haired girl blurred.

"Zach hasn't had much experience with language," Stel explained.

"Nor with apple fermentations, I'll wager,"

Tom Cole added, laughing. He refilled the Gunner's glass. "If that doesn't untie his tongue, nothing will. I'll have 'im talking like a GPC orator before the night's through."

Whaleman caught the gist of the exchange. He smiled at Stel and said, "Language is one of things losing to Solan progress. Language is making slow think, is making change from thing to symbol and back to thing before is thought complete."

"What's he mean by that?" Sofia blurted.

"He means he thinks in pictures, not in words," Cole translated.

"Well gosh how d'you know what each other wants, I mean gosh what d'you read minds or something?" Sofia commented, the words tumbling out in an unbroken torrent.

Whaleman was staring at her lips, a frown of concentration marring his usually smooth features.

Stel translated— "She wants to know how you communicate without language."

Whaleman nodded his head in understanding. "I am start skronk your speech," he announced. "Words do not begin and end, run in current, many words are excess. This is true?"

Tom Cole chuckled. "You've hit it, Zach. We like the sound of language. Maybe we pad it a bit."

The Gunner nodded and turned back to Sofia. "At defense academy," he explained laboriously, "we are taught language in early years, but emphasis is communication of thinking—of thoughts—not concealed by padded words. Work in defense command is more time alone—skronk?—or with automats. Emphasis is to think fast, communicate later. Speak to automats is with code language—skronk?—brief, phonetic precision, transfer thought with no error."

"*Skronk* is one of those code words," Stel added. "It's even gotten into *our* language. It means 'received and understood.' Right, Zach?"

The spaceman's eyes clouded momentarily, then he asked, "Right means correct?"

"Right!" Stel said, giggling. "See," she said, turning to the other girl, "there's a language barrier even when we speak slowly. So talk to Zach like he's a robot, if you want to make sure you're getting through."

"I am human," Whaleman declared.

Stel's gaze flashed to Tom Cole. She observed, "He *is* picking up fast now."

"And he's right, too," the Reever chieftain said. "Let's have no more comparisons of our friend with a robot. You *are* our friend, aren't you, Zach?"

Whaleman touched his chest and replied, "Yes, friends. No speak also compare Reevers and normers. Skronk no difference, same, like—all one."

Tom and Stel again exchanged glances. The big Reever said, "There is a difference, though, Zach. Oh, you're right—we are all one big human family—but there's a difference. People like me, and Stel, and Sofia—Board Island says that we are something less than human. That isn't true. It's the other way around. No offense to *you*, Zach, but it's just the other way around. Do you skronk that?"

The Gunner was staring at Cole with a thoughtful expression. He smiled suddenly and replied, "Is difference in what you speak 'dehumanizing.' Now you speak, Reevers less dehumanized than Normers."

"Exactly!" Tom Cole exclaimed. "Love of Mars, Zach, we're communicating! We're not *reverts*, that's what I'm saying. We are just *stubborn humans*. We resist this dehumanizing process. It's Mother Nature fighting back—do you see that?"

Whaleman jerked his head in a curt nod. "Like

early days of civilization. Natural exuberance of
uncivilized races not understood by those more
evolved, is race wars and hatreds and communication null."

Tom Cole stared thoughtfully at his visitor.
"Well, I don't know if that's exactly like same," he
muttered.

"Is like same," Whaleman declared. His gaze
swung to Stel, then to the other girl, and returned
finally to Tom Cole. "What like is life for
Reevers?" he asked quietly.

"Mars, man, you can see it for yourself!" the
Reever exploded. "We have no rights, no stock in
the Corporation. We're kept isolated like so many
mad beasts. We can't reproduce our kind, meaning
there's no such thing as a pregnancy permit for a
Reever. We're catered and condescended to like
mental deficients, tied here to Terra and commune
life. Absolutely no voice in our own destiny. Don't
pretend you never knew that!"

Whaleman smiled faintly. "I am Luna-born. In
most of Solana, Reevers are little more than
myths."

"Little more than *what?*"

"Myths, fanciful stories. Many Solanis doubt
that you exist."

"I don't find that too surprising," Tom Cole
growled. "Sometimes, I doubt it myself." He raised
his arm in a commanding sweep of the commune.

"Is like same," Whaleman murmured, dropping
his eyes. "I also am isolated, but in space. Tied to
Terra 10 and moonbase. And what is meaning of
rights? Of stock in corporation? What good? Zach
is have same like all defense commanders, is have
right to defend Solana, is same stock as AgTech or
EdTech."

"That's not exactly like same!" Tom Cole
argued.

The Gunner smiled. "Not exactly same, like this. Zach is accept destiny, isolation, rights, stock. Tom Cole is not accept. This is like not same."

"Your acceptance was built into your dehumanized carcass!" the Reever shouted. "Mine was not!"

Interested spectators were beginning to drift toward the table, attracted by Tom Cole's emotional shouting. A small brown-haired girl with glowing eyes stood across the table from Whaleman, gazing warmly at him. He broke the disturbing visual contact, looked uncertainly at Stel, then turned a penetrating gaze to Tom Cole.

"This explains Reever," he quietly declared. "You billet here, work here, Terra, garden planet, home of man, best in all Solana, and you speak not accept. Zach billet Terra 10 and Luna." His eyes briefly examined Stel Rogers/Brandt, then returned to his host. "Work there, live there, no human companion, often deepspace—but Zach accepts. Difference is accept, not accept."

"That's right!" the Reever acidly retorted. "That's the difference. You zingoes couldn't bring the machine up to the human level, so you decided to take the human down to the machine level. Well—" He scraped slowly to his feet. "Here's a human that ain't going down to no machine! Now you tell me which one of us is the revert."

Whaleman's face turned a deep crimson. It seemed that a cold hand was clutching his guts and his heart was pounding. He thoughtfully scanned the sensation and immediately diagnosed it as *anger*. He quickly controlled the reaction.

"Tom Cole is the revert," he solemnly declared. "Zach Whaleman is the *per*-vert."

Tom Cole's eyes widened, then he flashed a broad smile and leaned across the table to squeeze Whaleman's shoulder in a giant paw.

"Thank Mars, I've got a human being here," he said warmly.

Embarrassed by the sudden display of affection, Whaleman averted his gaze and turned to Stel. "Tom Cole is correct—right," he said. "Reevers have not good life, even here on garden planet. But is also correct, good life is nowhere. Reevers, Normers, like same. Tom Cole is right. Board Island is take away human, put in machine. But this is necessity, is unavoidable—this is only path for mankind." He turned suddenly to stare into Tom Cole's eyes. "What is destiny of human race, Tom Cole?"

"I'm sorry but I can't think of the whole human race," Cole rumbled. "You tell me—what is the destiny of the Reevers?"

Whaleman's eyes went back to Stel Rogers/Brandt. "Stel is not qualify pregnancy permit?" he asked.

Cole's eyes crackled. "Found something you can't accept, Gunner?" he said coldly.

The spaceman was staring at the lovely blonde Reever with an almost melancholy warmth. "Stel is maternal ideal," he said.

"Your machines say no!" Cole replied.

"Zach Whaleman say yes," the Gunner quietly affirmed.

"And what do the guns of Terra 10 say?" the Reever leader asked.

Whaleman dropped his eyes and slowly got to his feet. His gaze roamed the faces surrounding him, then he looked into the heavens. The blurred images within his mind suddenly jogged into focus. He understood the message which Stel had tried to give him earlier that day, and he understood the full significance of it. The Reevers were planning a revolt. As unutterably impossible an idea as this might be, as pathetically illogical for any mind other than a Reever's to even contemplate, this could be the only meaning for the fantastic events of the past twenty-four hours. Whaleman sighed and turned a pitying gaze onto Tom Cole.

"The guns of Terra 10 do not speak for Zach Whaleman," he murmured.

"But they *could*," Tom Cole said tensely. "Those guns *could* say that the human machine age is over. They could say that every human life is precious, free, and self-determining. They could say that pregnancy and childbirth is a decision for the heart and warm flesh, not for the mind and magnetic tracings. Those guns could speak for every man everywhere. They could—"

"The guns do not speak for man," Whaleman quietly insisted. "They speak for Solana."

"And who speaks for Zach and Stel—eh? Tell me that, Zach. No—tell Stel. Tell her she's unfit to bear children, Zach!"

"I am not a MedTech," Whaleman muttered.

"You're not even a *man!*" Tom Cole sneered. "You're a robot extension of Board Island, you're a—"

"Zach Whaleman," the spaceman clipped. "*Gunner* Zach Whaleman, TechCom of Solana's gunship Terra 10. Now I return to—"

He had started around the corner of the table as he spoke. Tom Cole reached out with a steely hand and spun him around as the other hand exploded into Whaleman's face. He was aware of moving through space before crashing down onto the smooth plastic surface of the pavilion floor and sliding into a table across the way. Pain alarms were shooting up from his face and he could taste blood in his mouth. He lay there for a brief moment of disorientation, watching the floating and distorted face of Tom Cole looming up over him, this superimposed over a vision of himself in a program error. And then the error-image washed away, and with it, the training of a lifetime, and the red heat of human rage took command.

Intellectual centers stood aside as animal reflexes brought him to his feet with the angry bellow of a jungle ape and again he was moving through space, this time self-propelled and homing-in on an image of instant hatred. And once again, he was on the floor, the surprised and perhaps frightened face of Tom Cole now beneath him, and he was battering it, and battering—and then he realized what he was doing.

With a moan of self-loathing, the Defense Commander staggered to his feet and swayed drunkenly over the unconscious figure of Tom Cole. Two men leapt at him and pinned his arms behind his back. A third stepped forward with a rough-hewn weapon of jagged plastic.

"Carve his guts out," sneered one of the men behind Whaleman.

The Reever with the handmade knife obviously needed no urging. His knife-hand was already swooping forward—but then something arrested it. Whaleman's emotion-fogged vision cleared at that instant, and he saw that the "something" was a grimly determined Stel Rogers/Brandt. She was holding the man's arm with both hands and shoving him away.

"Leave him alone," she was saying. "Can't you see, idiot? He's like us. He's proved that." She gave Whaleman's attacker a final push and whirled to face the Technical Commander of Terra 10. "Welcome home, Reever," she said and took him in her arms.

CHAPTER SIX

The Glitch

Communicator Hugh Gaitsweller stiffened in his chair at the Lunar Electronics Observatory and bent closer to the signal analyzer screen, then quickly cycled the Clarification Program bank for maximum intensification. His eyes widened and he immediately hit the relay switch to Moonbase Central.

A robot tone from his console announced, "Defense."

"Observatory," Gaitsweller snapped. "Telepic from Andro Point Two. Command audience."

"Skronk," was the reply. "Standby."

A human voice came in almost immediately. "What is it, Hugh?"

"Pulser from Andro Two," the Communicator replied. "I'm feeding it through the signal logic, but I already know—its intelligent source."

"Give me the pic."

"You're switched, take a moment for the logic. About thirty seconds more."

"How do you know it's intel?" the Command Auditor replied.

"It's a pulse and separation scan almost identical to our blindsends. Only this one is beamed our way, via Andro Two."

"Uh-huh, I'm getting it now. Can you clear that spacing?"

"I'm on max intensity now."

"Run it through again, and this time program a high null into the spacer backgrounds."

The Communicator frowned, then punched out a new program trace for the logic box. "Skronk," he announced. "Here's the replay."

"That's better," said the human voice from his console. A pause, then, in tighter tones, "That's positive, positive. Good! Do you see what I see?"

The Communicator had waited forty years to see what he was then seeing. He replied in a choked voice, "Confirm, confirm. It's a message from other life."

"Give it Command Broadcast!" the Auditor snapped. "Immediate!"

"Skronk," Gaitsweller croaked. There was not even time to gloat over his find. His hands were busy at the console, setting up a replay for the Defense Command brass.

"Good listening, Hugh," the Auditor said. "Audience off."

The Communicator nodded his head in silent acknowledgement of the simple praise and started the replay broadcast. The robot voice from Moonbase Central came back on to demand, "Frequency report."

"Universal frequency," Gaitsweller reported. "First shift, sideband positive."

Without a pause, the mechanistic voice came back with, "1420 megacycles plus shift positive, skronk. Report doppler effect."

The Communicator sighed and bent to his tapes. Somehow it did not seem proper that he be subjected, at this moment, to an interrogation by a machine. After all, he was the first human to receive a message from an alien world. There should be dancing on the spheres of Solana. After all these millenia, man had at last discovered that he was not alone in the universe. Or perhaps there should be wailing. Either way, Gaitsweller resented the routine reporting. He sighed and began his report. "Doppler readings follow—point one, quadrant one, spectrum four repeat four—point two, quadrant one, spectrum . . . "

```
-....--....-..--...-.......-
.-.....---....-....-..-.
.-....-......-.......-
.-.....-......-.......-
.-....-.......-.......-
-..-..........-.......-
.-....-......-.....-..-
-.-..-........-......-
.-....-.......-......-
.-....-.......-.....-
.-....-.......-....-
-........-.......-...
-..-..........-....--
-....-.....----..-..----
-..-.....-..........---
```

**PLATE I - PULSER TELEPIC FROM ANDRO
POINT TWO, ROBOT SENTINEL STATION**

Dot-dash message as received by Communicator Hugh Gaitsweller.

```
-....-----..-.
.-----....-...-.
.-----....-....-
.-----....-....-
.-----....-..-.
.-....-----....
.-----....-....
-..-....-.....
--..-.....-...
-..-.....-...
.-....-......
-.-.----.----
--..-----.-...
-......-.-..
--..--.-....
-..--.........
-.--.........
```

```
-- .-------------
----------------
-. .-----------
--.-----------
----------------
-. . .---------
--.-----------
----------------
-.-.----------
--.-----------
----------------
-.--.---------
--. .---------
```

PLATE II - PULSER TELEPIC FROM ANDRO POINT TWO, ROBOT SENTINEL STATION

Dot-dash message as arranged by Logic program for 15x30 Scan.

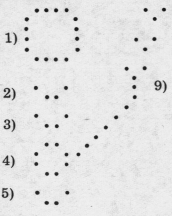

PLATE III - PULSER TELEPIC FROM ANDRO
POINT TWO, ROBOT SENTINEL STATION

Dot-dash message with 15x30 TelePic Scan,
dashes dropped, depicting Solar System (star
Sol and 7 planets) and visitors from outside
system traveling toward third planet.

Legend: 1) Sol; 2) Mercury; 3) Venus; 4) Earth;
5) Mars; 6) Jupiter; 7) Saturn; 8) Uranus; 9)
Powered Spacecraft (3). Outermost planets, Neptune and Pluto, not shown.

Ian Johns-Fielding, the Defense Director, paced
thoughtfully about his paneled office on Board
Island, returning frequently to gaze at the telepic
which was centered on his viewscreen wall. His
aide, Squadroneer Mark Bond-Durant, was staring
fixedly at the display while doodling on a small
magnetic traceboard. The aide had been present for
ten minutes, and not a word had passed between
the two men.

Johns-Fielding was 130 years of age. His
Homan-brown hair, wiry and close-clipped, was
showing silver glints at the temples—no other signs
of middle-age marred his youthful appearance.
Bond-Durant was half his age but looked old,
thanks to the genetic trade-off for the less efficient
Defense Command characteristics. He towered
head and shoulders above his superior and out-
weighed him on a ratio of almost 3 to 1. His face
was smooth and unlined, usually devoid of expression; his movements were fluid and perfectly
coordinated and suggestive of great physical power.

Johns-Fielding turned suddenly to his aide and

said, "Well, what do you think, Mark?"

The Squadroneer raised his shoulders in a light shrug. "Is standard teleview scan. Pulse is two to one, dashes to dots. Spacing unvaried. What else think? Here is alien message, long awaited."

"That's what bothers me," the Director said, frowning. "It's *too* standard. How would an alien mind come up with just that pattern?"

Bond-Durant twisted his lips in the faint half-smile of Defense Commanders. He was frequently amused by the Director's ignorance of technical matters.

"How else communicate?" he asked softly. "Frequency used is universal wavelength, is hydrogen emission rate. Is same here as anywhere in universe. All advanced life forms know this. Alien thinks . . . how communicate? Simple. Transmit on universal frequency. Use 2 on 1 pulser. If anyone smart enough hear, smart enough also to scan 2 to 1, set up scan pattern same, is simple elimination process. This pulser scans at 15 by 30, basic. Solani observatories also blindsend same pattern, lifeprobe program. Aliens hear blindsend, sure. Reply in same."

Johns-Fielding was again gazing at the telepic. "How long have we been engaged in these lifeprobe broadcasts, Mark?" he asked thoughtfully.

"Since twentieth century, speed-of-light type. Faster-than-light, only about eighty years."

"And we're still using this primitive dash-dot principle? Why haven't we gone to regular teleview transmissions?"

Bond-Durant again smiled. "Is require sophisticated logic-reassembly of teleview transmission. Dash-dot is more basic teleview principle, available to all advanced technological cultures."

"I see." The director was frowning again. "So we could not presume that this message was transmitted by an intelligence much inferior to ours."

"No, Defense Director, is opposite case."

"We should think of them as *superior* beings? Why so?"

The Squadroneer pointed to the telepic. "They know our solar system. We do not know theirs."

"They don't know it all that well," Johns-Fielding snorted. "They left out Neptune and Pluto."

"True, 7 planets only are shown. Missing ones could be Mercury and Pluto, the smallest planets. But this is insignificant point. Note telepic. Only bodies shown as full circle are Sol and Terra. Terra is third planet from sun, like same in telepic. This is significant point."

"I've caught you in an error," the Director said. "If Mercury is one of the planets missing from the telepic, then Terra would be the second planet and Mars the third."

"Apology," said the Defense Commander. "You are correct. Take my second point, then. Message shows Terra as Mother Planet of system. The otherlifers know this. They tell us that they know this. They plan a visit, in more than one craft."

"What else do you see?"

Bond-Durant shrugged. "In the telepic, nil. But . . ."

"But?"

"They beamed to Andro Two, so they have received our blindsends. They returned their message along the same route, not direct. Why not beam direct? Unless Andro Two is intermediate between systems, or . . ."

"Or what, Squadroneer?"

"Or . . . they do not wish that we trace transmission origin. They hide."

"Why would they hide?"

The big man sighed and leaned toward a communicator panel. "DDO to Lunar Observatory," he said crisply.

A coding tone sounded. Moments later the connection was made. "DDO request," the Squadroneer clipped. "Report origin, telepic from Andro Point Two."

An automated voice whirred back, "Findings do not correlate."

"Report findings," Bond-Durant snapped.

"Signal vectors follow," the automat dutifully responded. "Direction, first quadrant, seven degrees; velocity, light at the third power plus; spectroanalysis, signal source, red negative beyond measurement. Wave source does not analyze. Repeating, findings do not correlate."

Bond-Durant coded off the communicator and looked at the Director with a grim smile. "Our machines are overwhelmed," he said.

"What does all that mean?"

"Means that telepic traveled to Andro Two at third power of speed of light, straight down the galactic corridor, plus—"

"So what? We've been dealing with FTL amplitudes for decades."

"Puzzle is not velocity of signal, Defense Director. Puzzle is with relative velocities and paths of signal and signal-source."

"I don't get you. Are you speaking of that 'beyond measurement' business?"

"Yes, this is speaking business. Is Doppler shift of signal-source. Indicates that transmitter is mounted on system that travels at infinitely greater speed than signal itself, plus in opposite direction."

"I don't understand that," the Defense Director declared testily.

"Nor I. An unknown warp of physics is

suggested. If ships coming, and friendly, why not ships send signal? Also, *when* do ships come?"

"This is sounding more ominous all the time, Mark. Could that telepic be a warning from a third party? Of an impending aggression?"

"This is possible," Bond-Durant mused. "Now, question is, where are ships? Probes report no activity in corridor. From where do ships come? For what purpose?"

"The Chairman is going to be demanding some logic from us, Mark. We'd better get some ready. He has the intelligence computer mauling the thing around for him now. But he's going to want our counsel. What are we going to tell him?"

The aide shrugged his shoulders. "Apology, Director, no simple solution exists. Too many unknowns. Perhaps intelligence computer can extrapolate findings. This human is no computer. Can go on feelings, though. Computer cannot do this. Feel that visit is unfriendly."

At that moment the communicator toned, "Chairman to Defense."

"Defense on," Johns-Fielding reluctantly responded.

"The Chairman inquires if you have studied the telepic."

"Yes, we are studying it with great interest."

"The Chairman requests immediate conclusions."

Johns-Fielding tossed a half-panicky glance at his aide and replied, "Conclusions are pending final correlation of data."

"You have reference to the Doppler data."

The Director hesitated a split-second, his eyes on the Squadroneer. "Yes, and other considerations," he said.

The automated voice whirred back, "The Chairman advises Defense that correlation of all pertinent data has been resolved by the intelligence computer. Orders follow."

The Director switched on a recorder and said, "Proceed."

"Activate orbiting gunship Terra 10 with all possible speed. Deploy all deepspace squadrons along Defense Perimeter One. Allow no penetration of Solani space by alien craft. Station change for Terra 10 follows."

"Proceed," Johns-Fielding snapped, his eyes steady on the Squadroneer.

"Terra 10 will assume Earth-Moon orbit of maximum surveillance capability. This is all-speed, repeat, all-speed. Situation, emergency. Skronk-back requested."

"Skronkback follows," the Director responded. He punched the *Skronk* button on the communicator. The recorder began a playback of the instructions. Johns-Fielding whirled toward his aide and said, "I'll take care of the alert to Moonbase. You get moving on the Terra 10 end."

The Squadroneer seemed stunned. His eyes wavered momentarily, then his gaze sought the far wall.

"What's the matter with you?" the Director cried. "Haven't you been listening. I said to get Terra 10—"

"Apology, this is a glitch," Bond-Durant replied miserably.

"What do you mean? What sort of glitch?"

"Glitch is Terra 10. Gunner Whaleman is missing."

"Missing?" Johns-Fielding fairly screeched. "What do you mean, missing? I was talking to him not twenty-four hours ago."

"Affirmative, this is correct, and has not been seen since."

"Then put out a general alarm and, in the

meantime, get a replacement for him on the way."

Squadroneer Mark Bond-Durant nodded his head and walked stonily out of the DDO. He did not have nerve enough to tell the Defense Director that there was no replacement for Gunner Whaleman. Not without months of training and preparation. At the moment, Bond-Durant knew, Zach Whaleman *was* Terra 10.

CHAPTER SEVEN

Behold, The Man

Zach Whaleman, at that moment, was not so certain of his own identity. His uniform had been taken from him and handed over to a group of Reever women. Now, clad in only a crotchguard and plastic vest, Whaleman had to admit that he blended in very well with the other Reever men. He had been taken to Tom Cole's domehut where a cluster of men were engaged in a quietly animated conversation with Stel Rogers/Brandt. Dark looks were cast his way from time to time as the discussion went on and on. Whaleman, tied to a chair against a windowless wall, glowered back at them.

Presently, Tom Cole entered. A small plastic adhesive covered a cut beneath one eye and he was holding a contusion poultice to his lip. He removed the poultice long enough to grin at Whaleman, then went directly to the group at the other side of the hut. His deep basso quickly dominated the other voices, though Whaleman could not follow the line of conversation.

The reality of the scene was becoming more and more distorted for the Gunner. His mind had been in a continual spin since that moment of madness when he had tried to kill a fellow human. What could have possessed him? His mind quickly fled from any examination of Stel's amazing assessment of his actions. True—he had *behaved* like a Reever—but surely, this alone could not forever indict him as an evolutionary revert. The MedTechs had long ago cleared him of any such suspicions.

The discussion at the other side of the hut

ended abruptly, and the group flowed over to Whaleman. A big blond man bent over his chair, muttered something unintelligible, and untied him. Whaleman recognized him as the man who had piloted the gravcar during his kidnapping. The blond stepped back and delivered the thongs to Tom Cole. The Reever chief had been regarding Whaleman with a speculative eye. He said, "We don't have to keep you tied up, do we Zach?"

Whaleman shook his head and rubbed the circulation into his hands.

"I'm not mad at you, Zach," Cole said. "You did just what I was hoping you'd do."

"Apology," Whaleman murmured. "It has also been . . . like unreality . . . this time here. I lose reference with . . . correct action."

"No, no—you did just what any man should have done. That's what I was banking on, Zach. You've got real human genes down there in your center. I suspected it when you put up such a fight over at Board Island yesterday."

"Yes," put in George Hedges/Bolsom, the blond. "Some of the boys are still carrying your marks from that one."

"I am no Reever," Whaleman insisted.

Tom Cole released a sigh of frustration. He returned the thongs to Hedge and said, "Tie 'im down again."

Whaleman did not resist. He sat quietly and allowed the blond man to secure him once again to the chair. "I know what you want," he declared, staring levelly at Tom Cole. "It is impossibility. Reevers cannot take over Terra 10. Is impregnable space fortress. Is prop-dead, meaning no propulsion capability, must be towed. Guns are deadlocked, cannot be fired without resort to complicated overrides. Reevers cannot live long enough to unlock secrets of Terra 10."

"That's why we need your help, Zach," Tom Cole purred.

"This also is impossibility. Even if I *am* Reever, I will not give you secrets of Terra 10. Plus, Zach Whaleman is no Reever."

The blow came without warning, a jarring open-hand slap sizzling into the flesh of his cheek with all of Tom Cole's power behind it. The chair overturned and Whaleman crashed to the floor. Dazed, he lay there rigidly on his side and stared at the skeined feet of his captors. He heard Stel's voice raised in vain protest and a rumbling rejoinder from Tom Cole. Then he was being lifted, still tied to the chair, and set upright. Another blow landed on his other cheek and again he went over. A vortex was beginning to form in the depths of his mind and his eyes seemed to glaze over with a red film. He was uprighted again and once more quickly knocked to the floor.

As he was being lifted for the third time, Whaleman discovered that he was straining against his bonds and grunting with exertion. A tremendous animal strength was coursing through him, enflaming his muscles and setting his heart into a wild beat. His teeth sunk into nearby flesh. Someone howled with pain and a new volley of blows knocked his jaws loose from his victim. Whaleman was only vaguely aware of his own actions, and it was with some surprise that he identified the animal snarls and grunts as issuing from his own mouth.

An alarmed voice yelled, "Lookout! The chair!"

Whaleman's swirling head cleared briefly. He realized that he was standing and that the arms of the chair were still bound to his wrists, but the chair itself was in pieces and he was no longer restricted in his movements. With a roar of triumph, he willingly returned to the red glow of his inner rage and threw himself into the battle with renewed vigor, the plastic arms of his former prison now a formidable weapon as he swung murderously into the midst of his tormentors.

Bones crunched, and blood flowed and cries of alarm and pain filled the domehut, and then, Whaleman was moving fast through the doorway and into the darkened compound.

Stars twinkled at him through the sweet atmosphere, urging him onward. He glanced back to see Tom Cole and his men staggering after him. Whaleman had no idea whatever where they had concealed his gravcar. He quickly relinquished the forlorn hope of locating it in time and turned into the orchards in a hard run. Unreality enveloped him. Several times he fell on the uneven surface, and once he ran at full speed into a low-hanging branch of a tree, but he kept going without any thoughts of where or why. A long dormant center of Zach Whaleman had arisen in response to an urgent need, a very human and an entirely "natural" response of a life-mechanism in a survival situation.

His lungs were becoming inflamed and his legs leaden, but the Gunner of Terra 10 luxuriated in the new sensation. The sounds of pursuit were now far behind him. He paused to catch his breath and to rid himself of the chair-arms. His eyes fell on a metallic bar-like object which was apparently designed as a tool of agricultural maintenance. He hefted the bar in both hands, enjoying the feel of it, then slung it to his shoulder and jogged on. He had a weapon now. Let them catch him. Let them. He would *kill* them!

CHAPTER EIGHT

To Speak For Man

"Let him go!" Stel wailed, doggedly trotting along behind Tom Cole. "He isn't going to help us. You'll only kill him—and for what good?"

"He *will* help us," Cole replied. "That boy's coming out of his shell. When he gets all the way out, he'll realize he's in the same boat as the rest of us."

They overtook Hedge, who was bent to the ground and carefully running his fingers along the soil.

"Got his tracks?" Tom Cole panted.

"Yeh," Hedge grunted. "He turned up 33 here. You know where that'll take him."

"33 is a curve row," Cole mused. "Where's the nearest straightline?"

"I'd say 21," Hedge replied, rising tiredly to his feet.

"Oh, let him go!" Stel cried, stamping the ground angrily.

"Shut up that squalling," Tom Cole muttered. He took Hedge's arm, and the two of them jogged off on a slanting penetration of the deeper orchard.

Stel's gaze swung indecisively between the possible routes, then she made her decision and ran swiftly along row 33 toward the distribution center.

Whaleman was surprised by the sudden break of vegetation as he loped into the clearing of the distribution center. He dodged back into the cover of trees and dropped to his knees for a careful scrutiny of the unknown area ahead. He studied the high skyline of darkened buildings and listened to the faint hum of machinery and tried to imagine what sort of Terran activity was underway there. As he watched, an automated train came in low over the clearing and moved slowly to a hover-stop above the shadowed buildings, then settled gently to a docking. Whaleman understood. He grunted with satisfaction and moved into the clearing, swinging the metal bar like a walking stick.

Almost immediately a voice behind him hissed, "Gunner!"

"Don't go out there," the same voice urged, in soft tones. "That's Boob's territory."

This item of information had no meaning for Zach Whaleman. Crouched, the metal bar clasped in both hands and waving warningly in front of him, he was moving cautiously backwards, putting distance between himself and the Reevers. The men stepped hesitantly forward. Whaleman recognized them as two of the men from Tom Cole's hut. "Warning!" he cried fiercely. "Do not approach!"

"Can it!" the spokesman hissed, as the two of them continued a wary advance. "C'mon back over here. I'm telling you, Boob will . . . "

The man's mouth remained open, but his words dwindled away, his head elevated suddenly to stare at something above and beyond Whaleman. The Gunner followed the frozen gaze and reacted visibly when he found the object of the Reever's attention. A large beast was crabbing about just behind him, red eyes glowing, antennae curling menacingly.

Whaleman instinctively went to ground, throwing himself in a twisting dive onto the soft turf. He saw the pulse of the gun sensor and felt the jarring of air accompanying the ultrasonic blast. The two men had wheeled about and raced toward the trees, but both were suddenly flung to the ground in screaming seizures that brought Whaleman's hackles to stiff attention. Two guns were zeroed-in on him and blasting in alternating spurts. He flashed a quick look at the Reevers, shivered at their involuntary and obviously painful flopping, and whirled again to confront the monster, wondering vaguely why he himself was not leaping about the ground. In the corner of his vision he glimpsed Tom Cole and Hedge run into the open slightly uprange, then dodge back into the cover of trees.

Cole shouted, "Zach, get outta there!"

He stood wavering indecisively, loathe to continue facing the blazing fury of the autosentinel, yet unwilling to deliver himself into the hands of the Reevers. Then Stel Rogers/Brandt appeared, just beyond the flopping Reevers, and sized up the situation with a quick appraisal.

"Hurry!" Tom Cole roared. "He'll get to you soon!"

"No, don't!" Stel called out. "Keep going. Boob has no effect on you—just on Reevers!"

Whaleman was circling warily, waving his iron bar at the monster, trying to understand what was happening and to reach a course of action. Stel ran into the open, then reversed and leapt sideways as a Boob antenna quivered in her direction. The ultrasonic blast missed her by inches, and again she was diving and rolling, reversing and diving again, working her way toward Whaleman.

The Gunner stood locked in a reaction of shocked horror as the ultrasonic blasts continued bracketing the beautiful girl, then he came alive with an animal roar and charged the big machine, swinging the heavy bar like a madman, hacking at the spindly legs with the fierce gusto of a Viking warrior.

The bug whirled drunkenly, one of its legs smashed, its logic systems whirring furiously for a counter-program, off-balance and tottering as Whaleman began working on another leg. It tilted, all guns now firing wildly, and began settling to the ground on folded legs. Whaleman promptly leapt atop the automat, smashed the eyes, then—seizing an inspiration—forced the bar through a broken eye-port and rammed it in with all his strength. The metal bar flashed and sizzled and Whaleman was hurled to the ground as electronic circuits fused and exploded.

The Gunner picked himself off the ground and examined his tingling hands, forgetting them immediately as he swung to check on Stel. She was kneeling, several yards away, regarding him with an almost frightened gaze. Tom Cole and Hedge ran out to inspect the smoking automat, talking excitedly.

Whaleman went over and pulled Stel to her feet. "Stel is well?" he asked solicitously.

She nodded. "Except for slightly jangled nerves and a buzzing head," she panted.

"What robot is this?" Whaleman asked angrily, turning to glare at the wrecked autosentinel.

He released Stel and went quickly to the Reevers who were still shuddering uncontrollably on the ground. Both men's eyes were rolling in their sockets and their lips were foaming.

"What explains this?" he demanded, swinging quickly away in revulsion.

"They'll be all right," Stel assured him. "A boobing is painful but not fatal."

"What is boobing?" Whaleman persisted. "Explain automat attacking human! What is this!"

Tom Cole, approaching cautiously, replied, "That's what we've been trying to tell you, Zach. You wanted to know what life is like for the

Reevers. Here's another example." He circled
warily and dropped to the ground beside his fallen
men, checked to make sure that they were not
strangling on their own tongues, then gave Whaleman a gaze of undiluted admiration. "You really
zingoed the monster good, Zach. I guess I owe you
an apology. You're certainly no Reever." His eyes
flashed meaningfully to the Boob's quivering vic-
tims. "Otherwise, you'd be in the same shape these
boys are in right now."

"Boobing is only for Reevers?" the Gunner
said.

Cole nodded his head and tiredly pushed
himself upright. "That's our stock in the corporation, Zach. Delivered everytime we show ourselves
outside the orchards."

Whaleman pivoted defensively at the approach
of Hedge. The big blond grinned and thrust his
palms straight out in front.

"Friends," he said. "Anybody can mutilate
Boob like that is my hero for life."

"You're free to go," Tom Cole muttered. "Go
on. Go on back to your whirring machines."

Whaleman's gaze sought the outline of the
buildings. "Is transportation there?" he inquired.

Tom Cole sighed. "Go around to the other
side. You'll find a plastic walkway. It'll take you to
the manager's complex. He's a little gray Homan
and you'll probably scare the Mars dust out of him
at first, dressed like that, but I guess you can
handle that problem all right."

Stel had flung herself away and was retreating
to the trees. Whaleman watched her departure with
veiled eyes, then he looked at the wreckage of the
autosentinel, and finally at the fallen Reevers.
"Point is made," he said tiredly. "Need is, someone
talk for Reevers."

Stel had paused at the treeline and was gazing

back at him. Tom Cole stepped directly in front of Whaleman and extended his hand. "You're the only talker I know," Cole said.

The Gunner touched hands with the Reever chieftain, then followed after the girl. She gave him a warm smile and slipped an arm about his waist, and they disappeared together into the trees.

Tom Cole let out a whoop and hoisted a boobed Reever onto his shoulder.

"Don't tell me there ain't no God," he grunted happily.

Hedge picked up the other victim and said, "Well, at least, there's a Stel."

CHAPTER NINE

A Weakness Boobed

They were seated in a circle on the floor of the leader's domehut—Whaleman, Cole, Hedge, Blue, and several other Reevers. Stel hovered in the background, preparing food and drink. "Explain plans for Terra 10," Whaleman requested, staring fixedly at Tom Cole.

"We need the gunship for bargaining power," replied the big Reever. "That's all. We don't want to kill anybody or destroy anything. But we have to get their attention—and we can do that by taking Terra 10 away from them."

"Intent is to ransom gunship?" Whaleman inquired.

"Not exactly. We mean to hold it over their heads—as a threat. Give us rights and freedom—or we make war."

The Gunner nodded his head in understanding. "Could work. Maybe not. Once in Terra 10, no Solan power could reach you. In reverse, though, no Reever power could reach you also. Isolation is complete. Life systems aboard gunship are minimal. Food storage, small. Board Island could starve you out."

Hedge shifted his weight about uncomfortably and murmured, "We'd give them a deadline to meet. Come across by such and such a time, or else."

"Explain 'or else'," Whaleman said.

"Or else guns would start talking," Hedge replied, grinning.

"What he means," Cole hastened to add, "is that we'd knock out some minor item to show 'em we mean business."

"Knock minor item? Explain further."

Cole flashed a warning glance at Hedge and said, "Like a Weather Control Station or something. That'd get them excited. They wouldn't like to see a couple of ag stations shut down."

Whaleman was thinking about it.

Cole looked about at the circle of faces, shrugged, and said, "Or if you don't like that maneuver, we could seal off Board Island. Allow no traffic in or out. That'd get to 'em quick, too."

Obviously, Whaleman liked that idea better. "This could be effective," he agreed. "Plus, no need to activate gun batteries. Defense shield could do this."

"I guess I don't understand that," Cole admitted. "What is this defense shield?"

"Is system making Terra 10 impregnable," Whaleman explained. "Isolation shield is . . . Tom Cole understands repulsion principle allowing compatibility of matter and anti-matter within atom?"

The Reever chief shook his head. "I never got no education in that," he growled.

"Not important understand," Whaleman said. "Terra 10 isolation shield is utilize principle of energy-repulsion, is like magnetic field in reverse. Shield is deep one thousand miles—no energy, no matter, no anti-matter can penetrate, is virtual space-warp, is bend space around Terra 10."

"What happens when a space cruiser runs into that shield?" Hedge asked.

"Is deflection happen. Space cruiser diverts along lines of bent space. Like same happen when radiant energy runs into shield. Is diverted, around and beyond gunship. Even radio waves."

"Then what do you do for communications when the shield is energized?" Blue piped up.

Whaleman studied the small Reever with intent interest. It was an intelligent question, bespeaking more than an idle curiosity. "This is Terra 10 special feature," he replied respectfully. "Radio waves at one precise frequency and below specific energy levels are admitted."

Hedge said, "So the isolation shield keeps everything at least a thousand miles away from the ship. Suppose you were in a hundred mile orbit of Earth, and suddenly you turned on the shield. What would happen?"

Whaleman smiled. "Is happen, Terra 10 is suddenly displaced 900 miles into 1000 mile orbit. In contest with mass twice in size, plus larger, Terra 10 is give way . . . but maintaining 1000 mile isolation only."

"All right, consider this, then," Tom Cole said. "You're up there, orbiting at a thousand miles. Your shields are turned off. A space squadron is approaching, and they're within your thousand mile defense zone when you turn on the shield. What happens to that squadron?"

"Is happen, squadron is suddenly on new course, following curved space around Terra 10."

The Reevers began laughing and talking excitedly with one another. Whaleman shot a glance to Stel and received a reassuring smile. She approached the circle and leaned across Whaleman to place the refreshments in the center, the heavy mammala squishing across the flesh of his back and setting up tingling thrills. He instinctively reached for her and squeezed her arm and patted her hand, then released her as she pulled insistently away.

"Is love, like religious waterfall," he whispered.

The girl blushed. "Not here," she replied breathlessly. "Later."

Tom Cole had not missed the exchange. Solemnly, he said, "I think we're going to have a marriage when all this is finished."

"Explain marriage," Whaleman said.

Stel whirled quickly and returned to the food area. Tom Cole chuckled. "We're embarrassing Stel," he observed.

"Explain marriage," the Gunner repeated.

"It's an old human custom," Cole said, smiling. "When a man and woman are in love and want to establish a home and a family, they get married. It's an agreement, a contract. As long as they're both alive."

Whaleman swivelled about to peer at Stel. Her back was turned and she was busying herself at the food shelf. He laughed suddenly and said, "Yes, marriage. This is good. Zach will marriage Stel."

"You've got to free the Reevers first," Cole reminded him. "Board Island don't allow Reevers to marry—not even to each other."

"Board Island is not know of this marriage," Whaleman pointed out. "Is not known throughout Solana."

"Well that's just another of those things we got to get changed . . . eh, Zach?" Cole said.

The Gunner was looking troubled. "Is . . . is reversionary concept? This marriage?"

Cole was replying, "Oh, I don't think—" when a perspiring Reever entered the hut and announced, "We got the Boob out here, Tom."

"Good," the leader said. "Get one of those dummy huts set up around it. Then start taking it apart, piece by piece."

The man jerked his head in acknowledgement of the instructions and hurried out. Tom Cole looked at Whaleman and said, "I'm going to find out why that bug rattles my brains and not yours."

Whaleman nodded. "This is high crime, program machine to attack human. This is make point to Zach Whaleman, is prove Board Island not infallible. If mistake here, perhaps mistake elsewhere also. Is maybe mistake isolate Reevers, is maybe unjust."

"Maybe *Mars*!" Cole exclaimed.

"Let's get back to the plan," Hedge suggested.

"Plan is make simple," Whaleman said. "Zach will board Terra 10, no other human on board. Will energize defense shield and lock on Board Island, maintaining thousand-mile. Board Island is now in outer perimeter of gunship's isolation shield, island also is isolated." His eyes sought the Reever leader's. "Tom Cole must reach Board Island before shield is energized, otherwise isolation deflects Tom Cole, also. From island, no communication possible except to and from Terra 10. Skronk? Tom Cole talk to Board, explain injustice, get Reever freedom. Communicate with Zach from DDO. Zach—"

"Wait, wait, wait!" Cole said testily. "You're going too fast. What is this DDO?"

"DDO is Defense Director Office. Has only direct link, Board Island to Terra 10." Whaleman smiled. "See? Image-think is superior to language-think." He chuckled. "Tom Cole say Zach going too fast, unskronk, unskronk."

Cole smiled and replied, "So, the skein is on the other foot. But listen, Zach, I'm not so sure your plan is sound."

"I don't like the idea of Tom bearding the lion in person," Hedge worried aloud.

"What is *beardon line?*" Whaleman asked.

Tom Cole chuckled. "It's a figure of speech, Zach. He means it might not be safe for me on Board Island. I was thinking about that, too."

Blue put in, "They're not exactly accustomed to taking Reevers seriously. And even if they do, they might just grab him and execute him for his impertinence."

Whaleman was giving Blue a baffled look. Hedge explained, "Execute means kill—off with his head."

The Gunner's features were contorted in a grimace of distaste. "No, no," he said slowly. "Taking human life is high crime. This would not be."

"But just a little higher than torturing 'em with robots, eh?" Hedge retorted evenly.

"I have a better idea," Blue offered, "—if anyone wants to hear it."

"Blue is our electronics expert," Cole explained.

"Reevers have electronics?" Whaleman asked, in obvious surprise.

"Strictly underground," Cole replied. "We keep in touch with the other communes. What's your idea, Blue?"

"If Zach will give me that super-secret frequency for Terra 10, I'll bet I can duplicate it with the stuff we already have. Then we could beam our demands from here to Terra 10 and Zach could relay on to Board Island. Or maybe we could penetrate that shield right from here. How about it, Zach—could we?"

"If enough power, if not too much power, maybe so."

"Well, how about it?" Blue persisted. "Will you give me that frequency?"

Whaleman appeared to be chewing the idea. While he pondered, a man ran quickly in from the outside.

"A dense-air formation just buzzed over," he announced excitedly.

Hedge and Tom Cole exchanged startled glances, then leapt to their feet and hurried outside. The others, except for Whaleman and Blue, quickly followed. Stel paused at the doorway to throw Whaleman a warm glance, then went on out.

"How about it?" Blue demanded. "What's your isolation frequency?"

"Your equipment, what kind?" Whaleman asked. "Is FTL?"

"Is what?"

"FTL. Faster than light."

Blue laughed. "Don't talk to me like I'm an idiot," he said softly. "*Nothing* is faster than light."

Whaleman merely nodded his head, offering no further information. Blue stared at him for a moment, then said, "Huh? Is there?"

"For eighty years, yes," Whaleman said quietly. "FTL principles now widely used—communication, transport, many uses."

Blue was staring at the Gunner as though undecided as to believe him or not. A high-pitched buzzing sound passed directly overhead.

"They're back," Blue commented. "Wonder what they want." He struggled to his feet.

"*They?*" Whaleman asked.

"Patrol squadron, dense atmosphere craft—you know."

Whaleman knew. He had heard of the special DDO force, but never had personal contact with them.

Blue was moving toward the open doorway. "Guess they discovered the Boob is missing," he muttered. "There'll be blood to pay if they find 'im here."

Whaleman joined him at the doorway. The first hint of dawn was edging into the horizon. In the darkness, directly overhead, several powered craft hovered. A beam of light from one of the ships was sweeping the commune. The beam found Tom Cole and a large group of Reevers in the pavilion area and stayed on them. Cole was shading his eyes with both hands and glaring angrily into the sky.

An amplified voice wafted down. "Greetings to the Reever commune. We search for a missing spacecraft. Can you provide any helpful information?"

No response came from the ground. The amplified voice said, "Our receptors receive your very breath. Speak, and we will hear you. Can you provide information?"

Tom Cole roared back, "What the comet's tail would a spacecraft be doing down here? Look over at the distribution center, five miles due East."

"This is a Solan emergency," advised the voice from the sky. "Radar tracings indicate that the missing craft might have passed directly over your commune. Has anything at all unusual occurred in the past thirty-six hours?"

One of the Reevers in the Cole group sniggered. The tall chieftain quickly clamped a hand over the man's mouth and replied, "The days and nights of the Reevers are filled with deadeningly usual things. Go away. You frighten our women."

"I cannot overemphasize importance of this search mission," the voice persisted. "In the name and destiny of Solana, we implore you to act responsibly. We seek a gravity-drive spacecar assigned to the Gunner of Solana Gunship Terra 10. This is a Solana emergency. Please cooperate."

"What's all the panic about?" Cole rumbled.

"Repeating—this is a Solan emergency."

"Well what the Mars you want *me* to do about it?"

"Send your people into the arboreal areas, and search for the wreckage of such a craft. Report immediately any findings to your station manager."

"And get zingoed by the Boob!" Cole roared. "No, thanks."

Whaleman, still in the doorway, smothered an impulse to run into the spotlight and announce his presence. The inner conflict set up by this tug of duty churned his stomach and weakened his knees. Blue threw him a concerned look, then gently pushed him back inside the hut.

"Is Solan emergency," Whaleman grunted.

"It's a Solan emergency every time these guys come over," Blue told him. "Don't worry about it."

Outside, Cole was replying to another plea for assistance. "You get that zinging Boob off our backs, and maybe we can do something."

The amplified voice responded, "Please accept my assurances that the autosentinel will not attack you."

"You know what you can do with your assurances," Tom Cole yelled back—then, following a short pause, "Okay, okay. We'll look for your missing flivver."

"The Chairman will personally acknowledge your participation in this emergency situation," came the response. The beam of light disappeared, and the formation moved swiftly away.

Upon re-entering the hut, Tom Cole was saying, "I didn't realize they'd miss you so much, Zach. I guess—" He checked his words and looked hard at Whaleman, who was slumped into a bubble chair at the far wall. "Mars, what happened to our boy?" he asked Blue. "He looks *green!*"

"Be quiet, he just threw up," Blue replied in a low voice. "It's like he got boobed."

"Over what?" Cole threw a lightning glance toward the doorway. "Over that out there?"

Blue soberly nodded his head and watched Stel hurrying to Whaleman's side. "They got these guys roped up pretty tight. It's made me wonder, Tom. Is he going to be able to go through with this deal?"

A growl rattled in Tom Cole's throat. "He'll go through with it, or he'll die trying."

"Yeah," Blue said, "but if he dies, we all die—right?"

Tom Cole glowered at his small companion, then whirled about and stalked outside. Blue looked at Hedge and said, "I guess that makes it unanimous. We either swim or sink, all of us, together."

"We're already sunk," Hedge commented lightly. "The Gunner is the only buoy close enough to grab onto."

"That's what I said," Blue replied. "All of us . . . together . . . to the briny deeps, and faster than light."

"Faster than *what*?"

Blue frowned and moved slowly toward the door. "That's what I intend to find out," he muttered.

CHAPTER TEN

The Abort

Whaleman's uniform had been returned to him, more exact replicas having been made for a large number of the Reever men. With a feeling closely approaching guilt, he had donned the blue and black of the Defense Command and was examining himself in the mirror. A stranger stared back at him from the reflecting surface—an alien. A man who had been pledged to the defense of Solana since before his birth—and now plotting to undermine the authority of the governing board.

More than inner emotions were responsible for the distorted image in the mirror. His face was scratched and bruised and a large welt traversed his forehead—this latter, he surmised, a result of his run-in with the tree on the previous night's flight from the Reevers. His hands, also, were bruised and blistered—from his attack on the autosentinel.

Stel came in while he was engrossed with his tarnished image, moved up behind him, and encircled him with her arms.

"You are beautiful," she told him.

He smiled at her reflection and said, "Stel is beautiful. Our children will be so."

She released him and turned away. "Half Reever and half Normer," she murmured. "What will that make them?"

"I also am Reever," Zach quietly declared.

"That isn't true," she replied. "So don't say it."

"Is true," he insisted. "Only Reever could do what Zach has done. This is Reever proof. In doing, in thinking—not in appearing. Zach Whaleman is a Reever."

She was gazing at him from beneath lowered lashes, half-reclining against the wall of the hut, hands clasped across her tummy. "Boob didn't bother you," she pointed out.

"Is explanation, having do with Reever orientation in early life. Zach not oriented as Reever, thus not affected by Boob."

"How do you know that?"

He smiled and spread his hands, having picked up the gesture from Tom Cole. "Not know, surmise. One day know. One day, no more Boobs."

Stel sighed and moved her gaze to the window. "I've never been really enthusiastic about this venture," she told him. "I've gone along with Tom because it kept him occupied and . . . and seemed to give him a reason for living. But now that we're at the point of actually *doing* something . . . well . . . Zach, it frightens me. I don't think we'll make it."

"Make it?" Whaleman echoed. "Mean, not succeed? We will succeed—make it. Board will listen to Tom Cole, will understand, will change life of Reevers."

"Zach, you're so terribly naive," Stel complained.

"Unskronk," he said, aware that she was displeased with him.

"They're never going to free the Reevers!" she cried. "They're scared to death of us. We represent everything they fear. We . . . They—"

"Wait!" Whaleman interrupted. "They? Who are *they?*"

"The Normers—the governors and managers and—and your precious *Board.* They're scared to death of a good old balanced human psyche! Why do you think they've gone to such lengths to dehumanize the race? Why do you think . . . " She ran out of emotion and slumped against the wall, biting her lips, and staring dismally out the window.

"Stel also speaks of dehumanizing," Whaleman said quietly. "Is Zach dehumanized?"

Her eyes went to his, crackling with emotional intensity, then they softened, and she murmured, "You're a borderline case, Zach. Whatever you are, I love you—and I guess I'm stuck with that."

"Stel loves Zach Whaleman?" he said, suddenly beaming. "Like same religious?"

She nodded her head and dropped her eyes. "Like same," she said softly.

She walked into his arms and pressed her lips to his, pressing warmly into his embrace. The electric kiss tingled Whaleman from head to foot, and he was gathering her into an impassioned response when Blue entered the hut and stood calmly watching them.

Stel was the first to become aware of the intrusion. She pulled away from the heart-pounding embrace, smiled at Whaleman from the doorway, and went out. Blue said, "Every guy in this camp's been trying to get next to Stel. No dice. What's your secret, Zach?"

Slightly dizzied from his rampaging passions, Whaleman gazed drunkenly at the small Reever. "Secret? Yes, is secret, mystery, like religious. Zach will marriage Stel."

"Not unless you pull your oars right, buddy."

"Explain pull oars."

Blue laughed. "That means you have to bring the Reevers out on top."

The Gunner frowned, then replied, "Freedom? Yes. I will pull oars to freedom."

"You can't let yourself get boobed by those Normers," Blue warned.

Whaleman glanced at himself in the mirror.

"Unskronk. Zach is not affected by Boob."

"There's more than one way to boob a guy," Blue pointed out. "You got boobed last night when that patrol squadron came over."

The Gunner was staring quizzically at the little Reever. "True," he said presently. "This is important truth."

"You bet it's important. You have to get yourself clear off the fence. You know—you have to pick a place to stand and die, and then forget about everything else."

Whaleman puzzled through the cryptic message, then nodded his head in understanding. "Yes, Blue, I skronk."

"You can't let yourself get all torn up inside. You have to pick a side, any side, and then stick with that decision."

"Skronk," Whaleman soberly replied.

"You want to give me that penetration frequency now, for Terra 10?"

Whaleman reflected for a moment, then said, "Isolation frequency, yes. Is—"

He was interrupted by a sudden commotion just outside the hut. Blue's eyebrows rose, and he stepped quickly to the doorway, then hurriedly turned back to say something to the Gunner. Too late—Whaleman was moving quickly behind him. They collided, and Whaleman's larger bulk propelled the two of them on into the open of the compound.

Blue grunted, "Back! Get back inside!"

Whaleman was aware, however, that it was too late to return to the hut. Tom Cole, Hedge, and Stel stood a few yards away, staring at Whaleman with stricken eyes. A formation of six hoverscooters were idling in the air just above the compound, and already Whaleman had been spotted by the patrol.

An amplified voice of elation called out,
"Gunner Whaleman! Thank the Corporation! We
feared you dead!"

The Gunner threw a helpless look at Stel and
raised a hand in greeting to the patrol. "I live and
breathe," he announced. "But not thanks to the
Corporation. Thanks to the Reevers of this commune."

One of the craft was descending, angling
toward a spot directly in front of Whaleman's
position. Stel pulled loose from Tom Cole's re-
straining grasp and raced over to the Gunner's side.
He tightly clasped her hand and waited for the
scooter to settle. The other scooters had gone to a
tight-security formation, a polyhedron with zing-
guns covering the entire commune area.

The leader of the patrol squadron stood up in
his open-air craft and saluted Whaleman. "We will
also salvage your gravcar, Defense Commander," he
reported.

"I know not location of car," Whaleman
truthfully stated. He pointed into the trees. "I was
afoot, far away. Attacked by automat. Reevers
assisted, many injured, but destroyed automat."
He threw a meaningful glance at Tom Cole and
again addressed the patrol leader. "Thanks to
Reevers, I am here now, guest."

"The commune will be rewarded," the patrolman replied. "I am instructed to transport Gunner
Whaleman to Director Johns-Fielding with all
possible haste. Please come aboard."

Whaleman squeezed Stel's hand and turned a
look of frustration to Tom Cole. The big Reever
nodded his head in understanding. Whaleman said,
"First, words for Reevers."

He knew that he would have to be carefully
cryptic. The lightest whisper would be picked up
by the hovercraft receptors. He kissed Stel on the

forehead and said, "Stel Rogers/Brandt, you live
forever in Zach Whaleman's heart." He released her
and clasped Blue's hand. "Apology, Blue, reward
requested is in gravcar." His eyes emphasized the
remark, then swung to Tom Cole. "To you, Tom,
thanks that Zach Whaleman is now more alive than
ever. You must visit me, in my home, if the
heavens will allow."

The two big men shook hands, using the tight
Reever grip of friendship, and Whaleman squeezed
with unneeded pressure. Whaleman stepped toward
the hovercar, and Stel intercepted him with a
flying lunge, throwing herself into his arms with a
sudden eruption of tears. He kissed her tenderly on
the lips and pushed her gently away, then climbed
aboard the scooter.

The patrol leader made room for him up front
while commenting, under his breath, "You should
have been a GovManager, Gunner. You seem to
have won them over completely."

The craft was already rising. Whaleman fastened himself into the motion-arrestor as he
replied, "Reever mind skronks emotional formali-
ties."

The patrolman chuckled and punched a button
to bring the bubble-cover into place. Whaleman
waved to those below, realizing for the first time
how much *they* had won *him* over. The Reevers
were standing about in silent, dejected clumps.
Two or three returned his wave, and then they
were gone, the commune was gone, and the
continent was quickly disappearing beneath the
full-speed acceleration of the patrol scooter.

CHAPTER ELEVEN

The New Dimension

"Make your report, and quick!" Johns-Fielding commanded his aide. "I am supposed to be in a board meeting at this very moment."

"News is good," the Squadroneer reported, poker-faced. "Gunner Whaleman has been located, alive and well. Is this moment enroute to Board Island."

"Thank—! What is his explanation of the absence?"

"Unreported," Bond-Durant replied. "The Gunner reserves report for personal ear of Defense Director. However, patrolman states Gunner Whaleman rescued from Reever commune, North America."

The Director was moving toward the door to the Boardroom. "Bring him to me as soon as he arrives."

"Skronk." The big spaceman seemed to hesitate momentarily, then added, "Meanwhile, emergency alternatives continue re Terra 10. Should alternates be canceled?"

"No, not yet," Johns-Fielding snapped. "And, uh, until the Gunner has completely accounted for his activities of the past two days, he is to learn nothing of our present emergency situation. Skronk?"

"Skronk." Bond-Durant dropped off, and headed for his own office. The Director went into the boardroom, quietly took his place at the circular table, and tried to look unruffled.

A small, square automat sat on the council table directly in front of the empty chair of the Chairman of the Board. With Johns-Fielding's arrival, the other twelve chairs were now occupied.

A whirring voice issued from the automat. "It is noted that all Directors are present. Second Emergency Board of Solan Decade 33 is convened. Negative reports from action items issuing from First Emergency Board will first be heard. Report."

The man in the first chair, left, cleared his throat and clearly enunciated, "Agriculture, no negatives."

The man to his left reported, "Commerce, no negatives."

Johns-Fielding followed with, "Defense, one negative. Defer report for re-call."

"Deferment noted," the automat whirred, "and accepted by Chairman. Proceed with negative reports."

The director to Johns-Fielding's left began speaking. Johns-Fielding let out a quiet sigh and began formulating a delaying speech. He hoped that he would not have to stall too long, that Gunner Whaleman would arrive even before the re-call of his deferred report. He wished also that the Chairman would personally attend these meetings. That damn automat had a way of cutting right through stalling tactics.

"Technology, no negatives," another director was reporting.

Johns-Fielding fidgeted and made ready. *Damn* that Whaleman. It was looking as though Defense was the only negative in the house.

The Reevers stood around in stunned apathy for several minutes after Whaleman's departure. It all happened too fast. At one moment, they had stood poised upon the threshold of freedom and dignity—the next moment, their one doorway into that new life was himself crawling into a police craft and rising into the sky which had forever been denied them.

After an interval of shocked silence, Hedge noisily cleared his throat and muttered, "Well, that's that. I knew it was too good to be true."

"Now, just wait a minute," Tom Cole rumbled. "Don't everybody run right out and slash his wrists. Not yet." He turned to gaze speculatively at Stel.

Blue said, "I thought for a minute there he wasn't going to go with 'em. Then he just climbs in with a few jolly words and—and he's up, up, and away."

Cole ignored the comment and said to Stel, "What about it, girl? Is he coming back, or not?"

"I don't know," she replied in a faint voice. "It sounded as though he was telling us something else. But I'm more worried about *him* now than *us*. If they find out that he . . . " Her voice died away, and she gazed helplessly at her chief.

"Well, he left the gravcar with us," Cole said thoughtfully. "And he invited me to come up and see 'im sometime."

"That's what worries me the most," Stel replied. "If he turns in a false report about that car, and they find out, they'll—they'll . . . "

Blue chuckled. "Don't worry about that big Reever-in-disguise. He knows what he's doing. Did anyone catch the message he gave *me?*"

"I was getting around to asking you that," Tom Cole said.

"I've been working on him all morning to give me the radio frequency that penetrates the gunship's isolation shield," Blue reported. "Well, he gave it to me. I hope that's what he gave me. Said it's in the gravcar."

"So he *is* still with us!" Hedge exulted.

"Of course, he is," Tom Cole growled. He was

staring thoughtfully at Blue. "So what do you think he's planning?"

Blue shrugged his shoulders. "I think he's left the next move up to us. Look, Tom, he left us the gravcar. He gave us the radio frequency. And he, uh, invited us to call on him. How much more explicit could the guy be, with electronic ears beamed at us?"

Cole nodded his head. "All right, I been with the play all along, I just wanted to see if it made that kind of sense to someone else, too. Okay—so let's say that he's planning on seizing the gunship, just like we talked about. He's going to isolate her *and* Board Island. And the next move is up to us."

"Don't be too sure of all that," Stel murmured. "He's liable to get back among those Normers and begin seeing everything differently."

"Stel," Cole said testily, "I'm cutting you out of the council, right now. A woman in love isn't fit to make command decisions. I guess right now you're hoping he *won't* endanger himself."

Stel flushed a bright crimson. She said, "You can cut me out of the council, but you just *try* cutting me out of *any* thing involving Zach Whaleman!"

The chieftain dropped his eyes away from the coldly determined gaze of Stel Rogers/Brandt. He chuckled to cover his embarassment and turned quickly to Hedge. "Think you can figure out how to get that gravcar into open space?" he asked quietly.

Hedge nodded. "I been studying 'er. There might be some trial and error, but I think I can handle it."

"Blue?" Cole said. "You got any worries about the communications end?"

"I'll need some time with the gravcar," Blue replied. "I don't know why I didn't think of it myself. Her radio gear must have a channel on the isolation frequency. I just have to find it. No worries, Tom."

"Then let's start our preparations right now," the leader said. "Hedge, get the raiding teams together. Stel, see that their uniforms are proper. Blue, you check out the radio stuff, and then get someone busy provisioning that gravcar with food and water . . . and whatever else we might need. Hedge, go over that car real careful . . . make sure she's spaceworthy and capable of hauling a full load."

"I can't hardly believe it's happening," Hedge commented, grinning.

"It's happening," Cole assured him.

Stel said, "I can handle more than the uniform problem."

"Course you can," her chief agreed, smiling broadly. "You help Blue with the provisions, then you come over and sit in on our timing drill."

"I'm going with you, you know," she murmured.

"Aw, now *Stel*," Cole rumbled.

"I'm going," she declared flatly, and walked away to begin her first task.

Zach Whaleman marched stonily up the steps to Board Central. A tall figure came forward to greet him as he crossed the porch, calling out, "Ho, Gunner," in a familiarly mechanical voice.

Whaleman wondered if this was the way he had sounded to the Reevers.

He replied, "Ho, Squadroneer," and went on to touch hands with Mark Bond-Durant, a tele-circuit acquaintance of some years.

The Defense Director's aide inspected the Terra 10 Commander with critical eyes. "The Gunner has been injured," he commented.

"Is minor," Whaleman replied, being careful not to lapse into the musically conversational tone he had picked up during his short visit among the Reevers.

Whaleman replied, "Saved by Reevers. Attacked by automat."

They walked along in silence for a moment, turned the corner toward the Board's wing, then the Gunner said, "Repeating, attacked by automat. Comment?"

"No comment," Bond-Durant clipped back. He hesitated briefly, then said, "Zach . . . Terra 10 activation schedule is accelerated. DDO is redballed on non-performance. Action Item is negative. Skronk?"

"Skronk," the Gunner replied, staring stonily forward.

"DDO requires full accounting from Gunner Whaleman to explain glitch."

Whaleman snapped his head about and angrily eyed the Squadroneer. "Zach Whaleman requires full accounting from Board to explain automat attacking human."

Bond-Durant slowed his pace and pulled Whaleman to a dead halt. "Solan Emergency is declared," he advised the Gunner. "Terra 10 is negative Action Item. Skronk? Is redball for DDO. All else is minor."

Whaleman stubbornly held his ground. "Redball for DDO is not indicate end of Solana."

The Squadroneer stiffened noticeably. "Gunner will report all facts re glitch to Director Johns-Fielding," he commanded. "All else is minor."

"You'd better not bet on that, buddy!" Gunner Whaleman blurred musically. He wheeled about and entered the boardroom, closing the door on the aghast face of the DDO aide.

CHAPTER TWELVE

Strike Three

Zach Whaleman knew that he was on a collision course with his own destiny. He was fully aware that the unquestioned goals of his lifetime were now being scanned by the probing light of his fast-awakening intellect, and that the answers pouring out were far more disturbing than any considerations of corporate discipline. Not only goals, but values also were under attack by his new consciousness.

Many questions he would like to hurl at that Board of Directors—such as, "Why is man exiled from his own planet? What is the value of life without individual dignity? Was the race actually becoming dehumanized—and, if so, to what sane purpose? What was the net effect?" Blue had told him, in one of his casual asides, that the Solan population was becoming more and more antlike with each generation. Antlike? Was this the net effect, the ultimate goal of mankind? Mass specialization within a rigid society?

He would like to ask the Board, "Why can't I plant a son in the woman of my choosing? By what right do you impose pregnancy permits and restrictions? By what right do you bring forth new life with a program tape for a brain?" Oh yes, he would like to ask these questions of the wise ones. Perhaps, someday, he would—or perhaps, someday, the asking would be superfluous. For the moment, he would temper his challenge with the requirements of immediate need. Whaleman was, after all, a product of the superlogical society. Even his revolt would move along what was, to him, a logical line.

The ushermat announced his arrival to the inner chamber and responded to the immediate entry command by swinging the door wide and welcoming the Gunner of Terra 10.

Whaleman entered quietly and took a chair directly behind the Defense Director.

Johns-Fielding was staring gloomily at his own hands and speaking in a subdued, frustrated voice.

" . . . understand that, Chairman, but the human equation does not always confine itself to a program code. I am positive that Gunner Whaleman would have held himself in readiness had it been possible that he anticipate an emergency situation. At any rate—"

"At any rate," the automat cut in on him, "he did not. Do you deny the lack of human redundancy in the planning for this gunship?"

"By the Chairman's leave," Johns-Fielding sputtered, "the DDO did not participate in the redundancy planning for Terra 10. As a matter of fact, the training program instituted at Moonbase was not in the original planning package, but got its start as a process plan in DDO. Were it not for this supplementary DDO process, there would be no candidates available as backups to Gunner Whaleman. If the Chairman will recall, it was his conclusion more than 12 years ago, and in this very room, that the human system for Terra 10 was actually redundant to the machinated systems."

Whaleman was following the exchange with an attentive ear. On the several instances in the past when he had been privileged to sit in on such a gathering, much that had been said was totally beyond his language comprehension. This time it was different. He understood every word.

The Chairman's communications automat sat briefly silent following Johns-Fielding's lengthy argument. Then it whirred, "Skronk, standby."

The Defense Director turned to Whaleman with a smile and a wink. Whaleman inclined his head to the left in a formal salute. Several of the other directors were casting reproachful glances Whaleman's way.

The automat whirred again. "Presence of Gunner Whaleman is recorded and acknowledged by the Chairman. The Gunner will please approach the table, at his Director's left."

Whaleman got to his feet and went to the table to stand stiffly beside Johns-Fielding. "Ho, Chairman," he said, in his best mechanical voice.

"Ho, Gunner," responded a reedy and entirely human voice, through the automat. "Solana has been concerned for your safety."

The voice produced a marked reaction upon the assembled board members. Johns-Fielding's hand twitched spasmodically on the table in front of Whaleman and a chorus of quickly drawn breaths added to Whaleman's bewilderment. He had no way of knowing that the sound of the Chairman's own voice was a rare event which would not be noted casually.

"Apology," the Gunner replied stiffly. "Through personal error, I lost vehicle, was afoot and incommunicado on continent."

"That is understandable," the thin voice said. "I, uh, have this report here, Gunner, uh . . . you were found in a Reever commune on North America. Would that be Coleman/Seville's camp?"

"Is same as Tom Cole? If so, yes, this is right—correct."

"Uh-huh. And these people clasped you to their bosom, did they?"

"Yes, and these people are clasped to Zach's bosom, also. Chairman, Gunner of Terra 10 requests plaintalk."

Johns-Fielding's hand twitched again, and he

sent Whaleman an agonized look. Whaleman ignored him and listened to the Chairman replying,
"If you mean off the record, request denied. But
we all say precisely what we feel like saying in this
room, Gunner."

"Off the record not requested," Whaleman
said. "*On* the record is much desired. Chairman, this
human was attacked on North America by machine
programmed for such attacks. This human requests
clarification of procedure."

"You were not harmed, were you?" the Chairman asked.

"Not harmed, no, but Reevers were. In most
repugnant manner. Brains seized—bodies jerked
here, there—eyes roll, swallow tongues, agony is
suffered, illness follows. Request clarification."

"They got what they deserved," the dry voice
replied. "If they stay where they belong, no
molestation will befall them. Does this clarify the
matter to your satisfaction?"

"Chairman unskronks," Whaleman suggested.
"This is machine, attack human. This is put
machine dominant over human. Gunner Whaleman,
on record, protests this procedure."

Ian Johns-Fielding was tugging at Whaleman's
sleeve. Whaleman ignored him, his eyes fastened to
the automat for a reply. It came, but in the
whirring tones of machinated speech. "The Chairman notes the Gunner's protest and disqualifies it.
The—"

"On what grounds disqualifies it?" Whaleman
roared back.

Johns-Fielding's sibilant demand, "Damn,
Zach, shut up and sit down!" was magnified by the
pronounced hush about the table.

The automat whirred without speech for several seconds. Whaleman shook off his Director's hand
and stood firm, luxuriating again in the sweet

emotion of anger which he had first tasted such a
short few hours earlier.

"Disqualification rests in the Gunner's own
phraseology," the machine enunciated. "Words
Reever and *human* are not synonymous. The
Gunner of Terra 10 is dismissed. The Gunner will
proceed to Moonbase and present himself to the
Disciplinary Squadroneer."

"You've cut it!" Johns-Fielding groaned in a
muffled voice.

The realization crashed upon Whaleman that he
had pushed his point too far. "Request reconsider-
ation," he said thickly. "Request activation assignment, Terra 10, be completed before disciplinary
assignment."

"Request denied," the automat whirred. "The
Second Emergency Convention of the 33rd Decade
stands adjourned. Director Johns-Fielding will remain for special instructions."

That was it for Zach Whaleman, and none
knew this truth more sharply than did the Gunner
himself. He joined the directors as they silently
filed from the chamber. None spoke to Whaleman,
nor to each other.

These same men, the Gunner was thinking, had
warmly embraced him not too many hours earlier.
Whaleman experienced a dizziness as he reached
the hallway. He was not accustomed to emotional
stress and was finding the experience almost
overwhelming. He was guilty of serious error. What
was it Stel had called him? *Naive?* Yes, he decided.
Zach Whaleman was seriously naive. He had as-
sumed that injustice in Solana was no more than an
easily rectified program error, a glitch. He had
considered himself phenomenally fortunate to find
an audience with the almost legendary Chairman of
the Board. *Naive*, yes. And *stupid*! *Stupid* to think
that the Chairman had been unaware of the

monstrous machines that were programmed to attack humans. And now what had stupid Zach Whaleman done to his friends, the Reevers? He had set them up for certain destruction, that's what. They would never know that he had not intentionally betrayed them. They would be getting into that gravcar and setting a course for Terra 10, expecting a sympathetic Commander to greet them and welcome them aboard. Instead, they would find . . .

Whaleman shivered and leaned against the wall, squeezing his forehead with a trembling hand and trying to force himself to think rationally. A hand fell on his shoulder. He looked up, into the eyes of Squadroneer Bond-Durant.

"Apology, Zach," the Squadroneer said. "I had to report it."

"Unskronk," Whaleman mumbled.

"To the Chair," Bond-Durant explained. "Mandatory report, Gunner's Reever speak. Is Solan Emergency, is no time for doubtfuls. Come now. Also is time Moonbase transport."

"Unskronk," the Gunner repeated.

Bond-Durant was gripping him tightly and insistently walking him along the hallway. "Ease mind, Zach, is simple reorientation program. Much sex, much food, much rest. Maybe some Reever-screening, maybe some psych-test, some reindoctrination."

Deep within, Zach Whaleman was approaching an emotional crisis. He could not, he knew, allow them to place him in psych-out. Somehow he had to get to Terra 10. A dark image of Tom Cole loomed in a canyon of his mind. The guns of Terra 10, Whaleman knew, would have to speak for man. He understood Tom Cole now as never before. A voice was needed to speak for man. A voice which would be heard above the whirring clicks of the

Board Island automats. Terra 10 possessed such a voice. Tom Cole had known it. Now Zach Whaleman knew it. The problem now, he reflected, as Bond-Durant propelled him along the long passageway, lay in activating that voice—in reaching it—and in reaching it ahead of Tom Cole's visit.

He halted suddenly, clutching at Bond-Durant and bending forward at the middle. "Hold!" he croaked.

"Is sick?" the Squadroneer asked incredulously.

Indeed, the Gunner was physically sick. The crisis was now very real. Gunner Whaleman had been boobed again by the Normers.

CHAPTER THIRTEEN

A Gentleman's Deceit

Whaleman awoke to the canned atmosphere of Luna and the icky-sweet artificial odors of a medical billet. His clothing had been removed and he lay on a hard bed. The walls of the room were violet-hued with surrealistic views of Terra woven in. A tall female stood at the concave pressure-window, her back to him, leaning slightly against the window with arms crossed, silently gazing out upon the barren moonscape. She was nude, lithe and angular, hips only faintly swelling, molded along the classic lines of female deepspacers.

Whaleman swung his legs to the side of the bed and sat up, then braced himself on stiffened arms to keep from toppling to the floor.

The woman turned to gaze at him but made no movement toward him. The focus of his eyes improved as she unclasped her arms and dropped them to her side. He recognized her immediately as a Space MedTech whom he had known five years earlier, prior to his Terra 10 postgraduate assignment.

The Gunner's eyes dropped to a brief inspection of her chest area. Only the faintest swelling just behind the nipples marked the vestigial female breast. The nipples themselves were as small and tight as Whaleman's own and the surrounding flesh as hard and muscular. Unaccountably, a vision of Joan Mannson flashed through Whaleman's mind, to be quickly replaced by an image of Stel Rogers/Brandt. He doggedly shook it off and, in the process, lost his dizziness.

The Space MedTech approached the bed and took his hand, quietly noted the pulse-rate, then dropped the hand and said, "What happened, Zach? Why contusions, burns?"

"Afoot in Terra's gardens," he said dully. "Unskronk Terra."

The woman casually spread his legs and moved between them. She leaned against the bed and clasped Whaleman loosely about the waist with her arms. He ran both hands across her chest in an unembarrassed exploration.

"Where went mammaries?" he asked quietly.

She stared into his eyes for a thoughtful moment, then replied, "What is need, mammaries? Is evolutionary discard, this is where. Is Reever women not like same?"

"Some," he said. Obviously the SMT had been briefed on his adventures. He slapped her lightly on the bottom and said, "Why bare?"

She gave him the limpid sexsmile. "Need ask?"

Whaleman inspected the room with more care. It was a psych billet, he decided. She was pressing closer now, her fingers moving lightly and expertly along his back, and Whaleman was reacting physiologically. He lightly pushed her away and murmured, "Apology."

"Treatment," she whispered.

"Negat," he mumbled.

"Yes, libidinal alignment." She pressed in and placed a moist kiss at the base of his throat, then swept her lips up to nibble at his chin.

Whaleman was suddenly aware that some time had elapsed since his last sex release. The SMT, he also realized, was a specialist in libido therapy. He shoved her roughly away from him and said, "Therapy declined!"

"Zach forgets?" she persisted patiently. "Five-year is such long?"

Whaleman had not forgotten. This woman was an expert on masculine sexual psychogenics. They had met unprofessionally on several memorable occasions during Whaleman's undergraduate years at the academy. Her interest in sexplay was not restricted to professional applications. More than twice Zach's age, she had still not attained the median age physically but was still girlishly sleek of form and her beauty undiminished.

Yes, Whaleman remembered. The libido-therapist had been a sexplay artist for more years than Zach had been alive. Undoubtedly her accomplishments had grown even more during the years of his assignment to Terra 10. She was now rippling her hips suggestively, sexsmiling at him with a delicate tongue moving restlessly between parted lips.

He regarded her critically through his own mushrooming awareness, then his eyes fell and he murmured, "Not here, Helen. Psych billet is . . . depressing."

She quickly closed the distance between them, lightly kissed his lips and deftly massaged a spot at the base of his spine.

"Zach is ready, even here," she observed in a shivery whisper. "Not so?"

"Not so," he lied.

Again he pushed her away and lay back on the bed, turning his back to her. He felt her eyes on him through a long moment of silence, then he heard her at the communicator, speaking quietly to Medical Central.

In a moment, she returned to the bed. "Zach is prefer Helen's billet?" she asked softly.

He nodded his head. "Is more erotically soothing," he said.

She patted his hip and went back to the window. Moments later, another MedTech entered the room, removed a Defense Command uniform from a sealed bag, and arranged it carefully at the foot of Whaleman's bed. She stared at the big

Gunner curiously, gave some signal to the woman at the window, and quietly withdrew.

The SMT returned to the bed. "Know billet?" she asked.

"Same?"

She squeezed him below the ribs with a trained hand and said, "Same. Helen waits in billet, Zach. Come to Helen? Soon?"

He replied, "Yes. Is superior, Helen's billet."

She went immediately to a closet, donned a transparent smock, and departed. Whaleman lay unmoving for several minutes, aware that he was being monitored by inconspicuous sensors, willing his racing systems to stabilize.

As soon as he felt sufficiently calmed, he slid off the bed and unhastily put on the uniform, washed, applied the depilatory to his whiskers, and methodically went through the full grooming and toilet procedures.

It seemed too much to expect—were they actually going to allow him to simply walk away from the medical center? Either his stock in the corporation was a bit higher than he had ever suspected—or his aberration's were not quite as extreme as he had feared—or some game of intrigue was being played with him.

He opened the door and stepped into the circular lobby. A MedTech smiled at him as he passed the reception station. He went on into the underground tube and stepped aboard the mechanized walkway, rode it to the personnel area, then surfaced and walked beneath the plastic dome of Moonbase. He went directly to the transport section for an inspection of the spaceliner schedules, then returned to the tubes and took a pneumatic car to the spaceport. A hundred or so Lunans stood quietly at the shuttle station, clumps of Homans and Spacers, characteristically unmixed. For the first time ever, Whaleman took note of the herding-by-types and wondered about it. These people worked together—the Homan govtechs and other specialists side-by-side with defense techs and other Spacers—was there no basis for a social mingling also?

He shrugged off the thought and kept moving from group to group, remaining uncommitted to any specific egress gate. Several shuttles loaded and departed, each headed for outbound liners, but the crowd did not seem to thin noticeably. Whaleman was thankful for this. He scanned new arrivals, nodded occasionally at a familiar face. When the Terran egress opened, he moved slowly in that direction then made a last-minute rush and boarded the shuttle just as the hatch was closing.

He was the last person aboard, and he lingered at the viewport to see if any others had attempted to follow his late plunge. Satisfied that his movements were not under monitor, he retired to the pressurized lounge as the shuttle was falling away from the Lunar surface. The lumbering craft would require ten minutes to attain station-mate for the liner pickup.

The food automat came by, reminding Whaleman of his hunger. He took a beefpaste and apple-flake packet and wolfed it down, wondering vaguely about the time-lapse since his collapse at Board Island. He left his chair to inspect the Chron-Cal at the center of the lounge, grunted with satisfaction, and returned to his seat. Barely twenty-six hours had elapsed. Perhaps there was still time to save Tom Cole from a fatal mistake.

The warning lights began flashing. Whaleman fastened himself into the retainer, feeling the velocity pickup and then shift into warp speed. They would be mating up with the Mercury-Jupiter liner for the brief transience above the Earth-Moon system, divorcing six seconds later for a supergrav drop into the Terran envelope.

A steady red glow of the lounge lighting signalled the success of the marriage with the shuttle snuggled into a belly-bay of the liner. Time moved backwards for six seconds, then the lounge lighting faded to a muted violet and they were disengaged and hurtling toward Earth. The supergrav drive kicked in a few seconds later as they passed beyond free-fall and into magnetic acceleration. Whaleman released the retainers and relaxed into the reverse-gravity compensators of his seat.

Another five minutes, and he would be in Yorkport. He wondered if he was being watched and, if so, whether he would be allowed to venture beyond the confines of the strip city. He immediately rejected the thought. He was not suspected of perfidy—only of mildly aberrant behavior.

The SMT, Helen, was undoubtedly not yet alarmed by his delay in reporting to her billet. Whaleman experienced a surge of guilt. Helen was in for a bit of embarrassment, perhaps even severe censure. He dismissed that thought also. The discomfort of an SMT could not be measured against the fate awaiting Tom Cole and his Reever adventurers. He had to reach them, let them know that the plan had crumbled beneath his stupidity, prevent them from flying into certain destruction.

As a secondary item, there was Stel. Not that she could ever become a minor consideration of his life, but a rich lifetime still lay before them. At the moment, Whaleman's anxieties lay with the fate of the Reever militants. Even so, the knowledge that his primary mission would also allow him to be with Stel again could not be completely submerged in his anxieties.

Terra was rushing toward them in the viewscreen. Whaleman cleared his mind and concen-

trated on the view. It was one he would never tire
of. The fantastic blues and greens of this lush
planet! The shuttle was slowing for an atmosphere
entry and lining into the slot for Yorkport. A
barely perceptible vibration told him that they
were cycling over to Yorkport control as the
automatic gravity arrestors took charge of their
descent. Then the viewscreen was showing inde-
scribably beautiful towers of puffy clouds, and
they were flashing over the high mountains of
Eastern Europe. Fertile fields stretched unbroken
to the edge of the continent. Almost immediately
thereafter they dipped into the Yorkport approach
lane, and the great blue ocean was beneath them,
the floating fisheries whizzing by in a surrealistic-
like procession.

Why, Whaleman wondered, *why?* Why had man
risen from the only planet that could bear him,
turned his back on her forever, and sought his mad
fortunes in the black voids of a hostile creation?
Little time remained for philosophizing, however.
The egress light was flashing and the grav-reversers
were humming. In the viewscreen stood Yorkport,
and in the viewscreen of Whaleman's mind, AgSta
23 lay just beyond. Without a doubt, Zach
Whaleman was returning home. He was returning
to Reeverland, where he belonged. He hoped that
he had returned in time.

CHAPTER FOURTEEN

Film of Red

Whaleman moved out of the shuttle and into the swirling throngs of humanity at the spaceport. Even up here, he was strongly aware of the garden atmosphere, the sweet smells, the sparkling luminescence of solar radiation penetrating the wet gasses of Earth. He found that his appreciation of Terra's charms had grown, if anything.

He disengaged from the crowd and moved to a low parapet, sniffing the moist fragrance and savoring the smell of growing things which wafted across the spaceport from the fields just beyond. The city was an unbroken strip, extending in a straight north-south line as far as the eye could follow, no more than two hundred yards wide. One of the ten strip-cities of Earth, it housed and served the half-million Homans who were engaged in the vital task of food production and processing from the western half of the Atlantic to the middle of the continent.

Whaleman gave only passing attention to the unvarying architecture of wildly-colored steel and plastic structures, returning almost immediately to the line of greenery just beyond, his eyes moving quickly to the distant northwest and the deeper coloration of fruit trees. That was his goal. He rejoined the crowd and the swiftly moving staircase whisked him out of the spaceport and into the bowels of the terminal. He stepped off at the fourth subterranean level and casually approached an orientation booth.

A homan girl, dressed in form-hugging Gov-Tech gray, gave him the prescription smile and quickly inspected him for profession and rank. A single flash of the eyes told her all she needed to know.

"Terra welcomes, Gunner," she said pleasantly.

Whaleman nodded and then stepped back to avoid a noisy group of youngsters who suddenly crowded the booth. A male EdTech who was accompanying them grinned at the Gunner and apologized for their behavior. Whaleman hung back and allowed the GovTech to direct the group to the Andes Academy, a pre-professional indoctrinarium on the South Continent. When the girl returned to Whaleman, he was ready for her. He showed her a confused smile and said, "Terra leave, three-day pre-cycle, then deepspace two solar orbits."

The clerk nodded her understanding. "First view, Terra?" she asked.

He indicated that this was the case with a jerk of his head, adding, "Much confusion. Recommend tour?"

She stared at him thoughtfully for a moment, then replied, "Desire entertainment?"

He slowly shook his head. "Prefer, uh, view agriculture."

The girl's eyes lingered on Whaleman's flaming hair. She said, "Skronk," and consulted a light-tube display, then told him, "Some multi-season stations are open, Gunner. But no multi-crop."

"Fruits," he said, smiling.

She returned the smile. "Apples pretty. AgSta 21 and 23 are multi-seasonal, all operation in view at once—blossoms, growing, harvesting—even some planting now at 23."

"Request route to AgSta 23," the Gunner said.

She looked again at his hair, depressed a button and inspected another light-tube display, and said, "Know of Reevers?"

Whaleman nodded. "Indoctrinated," he assured her.

"Be kind to Reevers," she reminded him.
"Avoid if possible."

"Skronk," he said.

"If in trouble, anywhere in Reeverland, distress
call is *Boob*."

Whaleman blinked. "Skronk," he said.

The GovTech flashed him a smile then pursed
her lips thoughtfully while gazing about at the
various exits displayed on her tube. She murmured
an apologetic, "Ags travel rare," then raised her
eyes and pointed toward the far end of the
terminal. "Gate 66," she advised him. "Tube Two,
program mile post forty point seven. Skronk?"

The Gunner touched her hand, said, "Skronk—
gratitude," and set off for the distant conveyor
gate.

He was beginning to feel slightly giddy from a
new emotional strain by the time he entered the
tubes. He had left the crowds far behind, at the
other side of the terminal. This end of things bore
evidence of a creeping neglect. An empty tube car
awaited him in Tube Two. He stepped into the car,
studied the instructions at the console, then
punched the milepost program and took a seat.
The car began moving immediately and soon he
was hurtling along in a continually quickening
acceleration beneath the strip city of Yorkport.

Watching the visual display above the traffic
console, he took note of the point where the car
swerved westward, away from the strip, and into
the hilly orchard regions. Almost instantly the
annunciator proclaimed the approach to his station
and the car began a smooth deceleration.

The door beside Whaleman's seat swung open.
As he exited, he could hear the robot traffic
console cycling back to a homing code, and the car
was hurtling away before Whaleman's eyes were
fully adjusted to the gloom of the tiny tube-sta-

tion. He found the stairway to the surface and stood on the first step for several seconds before realizing that the stairway was not motorized. He began ascending under his own power and soon walked out into dazzling sunlight and the heady odor of apple trees in blossom.

A low-slung structure of var-colored plastics occupied a hillock some 100 yards distant, the only evidence of human presence in the incredibly lovely Garden of Eden. A small metallic sign emplaced just outside the egress door of the tube pointed toward the hilltop structure and bore the words "AS 23."

Whaleman moved quickly in the opposite direction, seeking the cover of the trees, trying to get his bearings and realizing for the first time the enormity of his undertaking. He had no idea whatever of the layout of the area nor of the relative location of the Reever commune. Then he remembered the words of Tom Cole on that last night when Whaleman engaged the Boob in combat. *"Go to the other side and follow the plastic walkway,"* or words to that effect. Tom must have been directing him to the station management, Whaleman reasoned.

He began a wide circle of the hillock, keeping it in sight and was rewarded some twenty minutes later when he came upon a narrow walkway of red plastic. Ten minutes after that, he found the distribution station. Several trains were at the docks, taking on cargo. The Gunner circled around the complex, keeping to the trees, and found the point of altercation with the autosentinel. It was still and peaceful there now. He wondered about the item of information passed on to him at the Yorkport terminal by the GovTech, thought about it for a moment, then stepped into the clearing and yelled, "Boob! . . . Boob!"

A duplicate of the monster which had confronted him the other evening immediately appeared at the other side of the clearing, moving swiftly out of the building area and scuttling across the open ground toward him. The speed of the ungainly automat surprised Whaleman. Here was undeniable evidence, to Whaleman, that the Corporation was officially aware of—and responsible for—the machine that attacked humans. Hadn't the GovTech given him the signal which would summon the monster, in case of "Reever trouble?"

The Gunner turned away from the confrontation and faded into the trees. The important thing now was to find the commune. Time was slipping quickly away. He went into a jogtrot, his eyes alert for familiar signs and marks. The unsettling events of the previous few days had taken a toll of his physical functions. He found himself tiring rapidly. His sleep cycle had been upset and his food intake badly unbalanced. He had expended large gobs of energy reserves, both physically and emotionally—as his exhaustion increased, his emotional deterioration seemed to become more pronounced, and he was fighting back a wave of panic when he came upon the stream through which he and Stel had walked earlier.

He let out a triumphant yell as he leaped the stream and ran full speed toward the clearing which he knew lay just around a low hill. Then he saw the flash of color of a domehut and—yes, yes—Reever Whaleman had come home!

He ran into the clearing, loudly calling Stel's name, then drew up short and leaned against a hut, fighting for breath and staring dumbly about at the scene confronting him.

Men and women lay in frozen curls, from one end of the commune to the other, some in the doorways of their huts, many in the pavilion area, as though some great calamity had befallen them instantaneously, without warning. A woman at Whaleman's feet was curled around a large serving dish, the prepared food scattered beneath and around her. A child lay just inside the hut which was supporting Whaleman. The Gunner knelt to examine the woman, found the lifesigns severely depressed, then he stumbled on through the commune, dazedly pausing to stare at a familiar face here and there.

Tom Cole's hut was empty, as was Stel's. Whaleman continued the now-frantic search and found Sofia Scala/Lowen balled-up at the edge of the pavilion. He carried her into a hut and carefully placed her on the couch, then began applying wet compresses and massaged her spine, diaphragm, and chest areas. He was rewarded some minutes later with a quivering solar-plexus and a muted groan from his patient.

As he continued the ministrations, Sofia began to uncurl, her eyes fluttered, and she began to weep in shuddering gasps. He kept at her, rubbing her limbs and speaking to her in soothing tones.

When he was sure that she was conscious of his presence, he demanded, "What is this, Sofia? What is happen here?"

"S-sick," she moaned. "Ohhh . . . sick—Zach?"

"Yes, is Zach. What is happen here, Sofia?"

"B-boobed. From the s-sky."

Whaleman angrily exclaimed, "Damn these Boobs! When is happen? Where is Tom, Stel, others?"

"Aren't they with you?" the tortured girl groaned.

"With Zach? No. No . . . Sofia! How much time is gone?"

Sofia drew her knees toward her stomach and

retched. Whaleman held her head and hastily
moved a basin into place. When she had finished,
she lay back in a more relaxed manner and said
weakly, "I think I'm okay now."

"Yes, Sofia looking better, more color, like
same before. Sofia, is important—how much time is
Tom gone?"

"I-I don't know," the girl mumbled. "A-
bout . . . I don't know . . . a few hours before
the . . . scooters came back."

"Morning? Night? When?"

"Ohhh. Let's see. Morning. Uh-huh, morning.
Dawn, Zach. They left at *dawn*."

Whaleman groaned and passed a hand wearily
across his eyes. "Stel went with Tom Cole?" he
asked presently.

"Yes. She went. Gravcar. Team One. Left at
dawn."

Shaking inwardly, Whaleman said, "Sofia A-OK
now. Rest, feel better. Then help others. Cold
compresses, Sofia-skronk? Massage arms, legs,
break neural blocks. Skronk?"

"I know what to do," she replied faintly.

Whaleman ran out of the hut, halted indecisively for a moment, then raced back through the
compound and the stricken Reevers. *Dear God of
the Galaxies*, he cried into the depths of himself,
find me a way—find my way to Terra 10!

On a dead run for the distribution station, he
tried to calm his tumbling mind and select a logical
course of action. Before long, he had decided that
no logical course existed. So—he would have to be
illogical! As illogical as *any Reever* could be! And as
daring, as determined, and as deadly. Yes! He
would find his way!

He ran out into the clearing at the distribution
center and did not slow down when Boob came
out to meet him but kept a straightline course

along the shortest route to the other side.

Boob did not slow, either, and fired at full speed. The blast caught the Gunner at mid-stride and hurled him to the ground. He came to a halt poised on one knee, hands lifted in surprise and pain to his head, and his immediate impulse was to scream at the limit of his lungs. *Why now were the Boob guns affecting him?* He instinctively threw himself to one side, dodging the way Stel had done earlier, and picked up another fringe-area reverb. This time, he did cry out with the incredible, sickening agony and looked about for an avenue of escape. There was none—except—perhaps . . .

With the desperation of the frightening responsibility on his shoulders for the lives of his beloved Stel and Tom Cole's raiders, he threw himself straight at the big bug, managed to grasp a spindly leg, and twisted wildly beneath the flat belly. The zing-guns stopped their ultra-sonic song and Boob whirled in frustration, sensors cycling in a determined search for the prey. Whaleman was on his feet and whirling with him, partially suspended with outstretched hands hanging on grimly to two of the six legs.

How long, he wondered, *could he hang on?* And while he hung there in temporal safety, what was happening to Stel and Tom Cole? He lost the grip of one hand and fell to the turf, then scampered back beneath the belly just as a zing-gun was depressing toward him. The Boob's intelligence bank was beginning to understand the situation. He stopped his whirling dance and idled, assimilating the intelligence. Whaleman took advantage of the lull to strengthen his grip on the legs and to attain a better balance. And then the frail legs began to fold and Gunner Whaleman began running out of space. The Boob was going to ground.

CHAPTER FIFTEEN

A Rage to Kill

Hedge was tensed over the controls of the gravcar, Blue beside him poring over an illustrated manual for the nav-comm system, and Tom Cole fidgeting at the far side of the command seat. Cole muttered, "Something is sure as Mars wrong here, mister, I'll tell you that for sure."

"Well I know that's Board Island down there," Hedge insisted. "There just isn't another place like it in the world. That's *her.* "

"Didn't say it wasn't," Cole rumbled. "Said something's wrong. And something *is.* "

Blue threw the manual at his feet and declared, "Well, that gunship ought to be exactly where we're at now—that is, if he's going to fringe the isolation shield down onto Board Island.

"I'm telling you, that's *her!*" Hedge said angrily.

Stel leaned over from the seat behind them and said, "It's the first time we've seen things from this height, Hedge. How can you be so sure?"

"I'm sure, don't worry about it," he growled.

"So where is Terra 10?" Blue asked calmly.

"That damn Zach," Hedge said.

Stel said, "Don't be so quick to—"

"Everybody shut up!" Tom Cole roared.

Stel threw him a reproachful glare and settled back into her seat. Hedge stared morosely at the controls of the gravcar. Blue retrieved the manual and began rapidly flipping the pages.

"Guess it's going to be up to me," Blue groused. He flashed an irritated glance at Hedge, then smiled, winked at Tom Cole, and said, "Look at old Hedge. The dream of a lifetime come true . . . and look at 'im."

Hedge snickered, pushed the drive lever into GRAV DISENGAGE, and sent the little craft falling into deeper space.

"May as well look around some," he said, suddenly grinning. "I guess we can cruise around up here until we're too old and feeble to ever take a gunship."

"Hurry and figure out that nav-comm, Blue," Cole demanded. "I don't like this flying around up here by the seat of Hedge's pants."

Blue nodded and replied, "I think I . . . might have something here, Tom. Let's see . . . well, damn—damn, Tom, why didn't I think of that?"

"Think of what?"

"A homer! Old Zach's got a homer on this baby!"

"What's a homer?" Cole asked interestedly.

"It's an automated navigation feature. If I can figure out how to activate it, it'll fly us straight to Terra 10!"

"No matter where she is?" Hedge asked.

"Well, I . . . yeah, I think so. Everybody shut up for a minute, and let me see if I can't figure this thing out."

"Maybe we should try to communicate with Zach first," Stel said. "Maybe he's had to change the plan—or delay it for some reason."

"And maybe he's had a change of heart," Hedge added.

Blue said, "I thought you were all going to be quiet for a minute."

"We are, Blue," Tom Cole assured him. "You just figure that thing out. We're going visiting Mr. Zach Whaleman whether he's changed his heart or not."

"Zach wouldn't do that," Stel murmured.

"Shut up, will you just shut up?" Blue cried. "I'm reading a hundred years beyond myself . . .

will you shut up and let me concentrate?"

Stel withdrew to her corner of the cabin and brooded in silence. They should wait, she was thinking. If things were not right, then it was for a good reason. And it would have nothing to do with Zach's faint-heartedness or treachery.

She raised her eyes to a fast inspection of the grim faces about her. What did they know, these poor grounded earthlings, about intrigue in outer space? If Zach had been a babe down in the woods, then all these were doubly-babes in the black reaches of space. She wished Zach could have come with them. *Oh Zach, Zach, where are you? Come and find us, my darling, and lead us from this blackness!*

Zach Whaleman was having disturbing problems of his own. The autosentinel had folded all its legs except the two immediately occupying Zach's attention. He stood like a Samson, straining valiantly at the two columns of the temple—except that Zach was trying to keep the temple up, not bring it down, and he was fighting a losing battle against pneumatic superiority.

Just as he was about to concede the fight, leap clear, and take his chances with the zing-guns, an amplified voice floated down to him from above. "You're getting to be a full time job, Gunner," it said.

"Identity!" Whaleman grunted from beneath the Boob.

The autosentinel's legs were straightening. The voice from the sky advised Whaleman, "Relax, Gunner, I'm overriding his logic now. Let go and step clear."

Another second and Whaleman would have been forced to do so in any event. His arms were leaden, his chest ached, head was pounding. He

stepped warily into the open on trembly legs,
fighting for breath, and watched the autosentinel
scuttle off toward the buildings.

A small, two-man gravcar settled gently to the
turf, the hatch popped open, and the patrolman
who had lifted him out of the commune raised
head and shoulders into view. Whaleman glared at
him, wondering if he could succeed in a break-and-
run. He quickly dismissed the idea. He was too
exhausted to breathe. Running was utterly out of
the question.

The patrolman said, "Well, Gunner? Will you
join me?"

Whaleman had to admit defeat. He moved
wearily to the scout car and leaned against the
fuselage, trying to get his breathing under control.

"Get in," the patrolman demanded.

"Sec," the Gunner replied. "Get breath."

"Breath to run with?"

Whaleman tiredly shook his head. "Breath to
get in with," he gasped.

The man chuckled.

Whaleman threw him a murderous look and
said, "How override Boob?"

"He's one of my babies," the other replied.
"He used to be on your side, Gunner. What
happened? The Reevers sell you a bill of goods?"

"Unskronk," Whaleman wheezed. "Unskronk
also Zach's reaction to zing-gun. Last time, no
reaction. This time, boobed."

"Naw, you didn't get a full dose," the man said
conversationally. "You better be glad you didn't,
Gunner. You'd be flopping all over this field."

"Unskronk."

The man chuckled again. "They popped a
half-wave microdot into your brain last night, up at
the MedCen. I recommended a full-wave, but they
wouldn't go for it."

"Unskronk," Whaleman said.

"I guess you never will. I don't skronk you, either, spacer. Everything in the universe going for you, and you toss it all. For what? For a piece of uninhibited Reever ass?"

Whaleman's breathing system, among other things, was clearing. He understood the significance of the patrolman's words and, even more, of his disrespectful tone of voice. The die was cast for Zach Whaleman. There was no turning back now, no place to return to, and nothing of value in his destiny that he could not make with his own hands and mind.

The patrolman was grinning down at a defeated man, a high one of the deepspace command, fallen from the stars to wrestle in the dust of Terra with his master—machine. "Come on, Whaler/Mannson, let's go," he commanded.

Whaleman understood the identity-change, also. He lifted his eyes to the patrolman and said, quietly, "Reevers in commune, all blasted, all . . . women, children, like same. You?"

The patrolman seemed to be enjoying his newfound superiority over a defense commander. "We promised them a reward, didn't we?" he said.

Suddenly Whaleman was seeing the man through a red film of rage. He cried, "Is Board Island know this?"

"Look, buddy, I get my orders straight from the Chairman." The patrolman's hand came up over the edge of the hatch and it was holding a small weapon. "Come on, enough smalltalk. They're pretty anxious to see you up at Moonbase. It doesn't matter to me if I take you back without a mind. You better climb in while you still got one."

Whaleman felt ready. His strength, boosted by a towering new rage, was flowing back and his breathing was steady. The patrolman moved back slightly to make room. Whaleman's other hand shot up and clamped down on the weapon, twisting and pulling in the same motion. The patrolman clung grimly to the weapon and flailed at Whaleman's face with his free hand. Slowly, surely, Whaleman's superior size and weight prevailed and the man was dragged across the lip of the hatch and to the ground. A bone crunched and the weapon passed into Whaleman's possession.

The man groaned, "Look, you're crazy, you're—"

Whaleman brought the blow arcing up from his heels. It exploded into the patrolman's face with a soul-satisfying splattering of cartilage and tissue. Blood erupted onto Whaleman's uniform as his victim toppled backwards into an unconscious heap. The deepspacer of Terra 10 and Moonbase felt a strong affinity with the long-extinct jungle apes who had pounded their chests in a victory cry over their enemies. He felt like doing it himself. Instead, he tucked the little Z-gun into his sleeve and climbed into the gravcar.

Seconds later, Whaleman was hurtling straight up into thin atmosphere while running a routine checkout of the control features. Satisfied that the tiny car was capable of deepspace flight, he kicked in the supergrav reversers and lined up on Vega. He had heard enough at Board Island the previous day to have a fair idea of the new route to Terra 10. Was that only yesterday?

Whaleman smiled grimly and punched in a code to the guidance computer. He had, after twenty-five years of life, only recently discovered the true delights of Mother Earth. As wonderful as all that could be, this was his true element, up here, in the great void. He might be a jungle ape down there. Up here, he was *The Gunner*—and he knew all the innermost secrets of the most terrible weapon in existence. Whaler/Mannson, eh? All right, he thought. That makes it clean and neat, with no guilt and perfidy as companions. The Reevers, in the name of man, were taking over Terra 10. *The guns* of Terra 10!

CHAPTER SIXTEEN

Babes in the Night

Squadroneer Mark Bond-Durant was not at all happy with the way things had twisted. He paced over to Johns-Fielding's broad window, hands clasped tightly behind his back, and peered broodingly onto the artificial scenery of Board Island. "This is terrible," he said. "A Gunner of Defense Command being hunted like wild animal. There is no justification for this, Director."

"Let's leave that, ah, judgment to those best qualified to pass on it," Johns-Fielding replied drily. "The uppermost question in my mind is, of course, Terra 10. Where do we stand in the activation proceedings?"

Characteristically, Bond-Durant's analog-type thought processes were leaping far beyond the reaches of the Director's Homan capabilities. He slapped his palms together and said, "This is also concern, like same. And now the best animal is chased across Terra, not guiding performance of deepspace frontline."

"Decode that for me," Johns-Fielding snapped irritably.

"Terra 10 is machine, is run by machine, and this machine is run by machine. Whole purpose of Defense Command is inject human equation into rigid machine systems. *Of course*, Zach is upset by machine ruling human. Does Terra 10 rule Gunner? Course not, course not."

"What does this have to do with—?"

"Has to do, like so! Zach Whaleman is no Reever . . . is *Gunner*, *ruler* of Terra 10. No man knows more, importance of human mind over rigid machine systems. Now . . . Zach makes protest, like same reverse, rigid machine *is* ruling humans. *No* Defense Commander can accept this—no, not one. Not this one. This does not make Mark Bond-Durant *Reever*. Like same, Zach Whaleman."

Johns-Fielding covered his confusion with a droll smile. "But you are the one, Mark, who alerted the Chairman to Whaleman's anomalous behavior."

"Error," the Squadroneer admitted, turning back to the window. "Would not do same now. Skronk, now, background to Zach's behavior."

"But it seems that the Chairman was correct, after all," the Director pointed out. "Whaleman did break confinement, and this is the only reason he is being hunted now. Our greatest concern now, Mark—and the Chairman's, incidentally, is the status of Terra 10."

Bond-Durant sighed and tried again. "This is like same," he said quietly. "Chairman is also think like machine. What is first priority, Director? What is prime concern of all Solana in this moment? Is visit from beyond Andro—correct? Is possible aggressive trespass of Solan envelope by hostile life. Is Terra 10 ready for possible threat? No, Director, Terra 10 is not ready. The machine's master is hunted across Terra like animal. Terra 10 is not ready."

The color had drained from Johns-Fielding's face. "But you assured me to the contrary. You told me that—that . . . "

"I told, alternate procedures are activated. This does not tell that alternate procedures are equal to full task. Alternates could perform routine functions while *maestro* is temporarily absent. *But*, Director, *maestro* is needed for ultimate implementation of defense plan."

"You told me that Whaleman's replacement was aboard the gunship *twelve hours* ago!"

"Correction, Director, I tell that Whaleman's *substitute* is aboard."

The Defense Director gnawed on his lower lip. "What do you advise I do, Mark?" he asked quietly.

"Restore Gunner Whaleman's command, soonest."

"How can we do that?" Johns-Fielding cried. "The man has broken confinement! We can't even find him, let alone restore his command!"

"He will be found. Recommend full search, North America first. Emergency broadcasts. Announce complete exoneration, Gunner Whaleman. Broadcast instructions, Whaleman reports to Terra 10 soonest."

"It was suspected that he might seek out the Reevers again," the Director mused. "We could sweep the area with hovercars." A sudden thought jarred him. His hand jerked, and he turned startled eyes to his aide. "Oh, *no!*" he groaned.

"What is?"

"The medics implanted an ultrasonic receptor in Whaleman's brain."

"Is *what?*"

The Director leapt to his feet. "Give it to me straight and quick, Mark. How bad do we really need Whaleman on that gunship?"

The Squadroneer raised his hands to shoulder level and let them fall back to his side. "Like same, Director, how bad is really need gunship?"

Johns-Fielding's hand clawed toward the communicator panel. "This is going to make me look awfully silly to the Chairman," he said. "But . . . here goes nothing."

Blue was explaining, "See, the homer reacts to a microwave pulser from a beacon on the gunship. But we have to trigger the beacon with a special command code from our nav system. Now, it says—"

"You got that code?" Tom Cole interrupted.

"Well, it's supposed to be all set up. See that little box right there at your left knee, Hedge? That's the baby. When the other systems are properly meshed, you just have to push that button, and we're on our way."

"So let's get it pushed and on our way," Cole said.

"No, it's not that easy," Blue told him. "You see, we got to—"

"I don't like it!" Hedge protested. "I got this thing handling right now. How do I know what's going to happen when I turn it over to the robot?"

"It'll happen just like it says in the book, Hedge," Blue replied disgustedly.

"How do you know that? How do you know that it won't zap us right into that gunship at warp speed?"

Stel commented, from the other seat, "We have to have faith in something, I guess."

Hedge retorted, "Look who's preaching faith in a machine!"

"It's a machine that brought us up here," the girl pointed out. "Or did you suddenly sprout invisible wings?"

Tom Cole laughed. "Stel's right, as usual. Give the machine its due credit, Hedge. Go on, Blue. Tell 'im what to do."

Blue said, "We first have to isolate on a field of attraction. Where's the moon, Hedge?"

"Ask Stel," Hedge grunted. He relented, chuckled, and added, "Aw, it's down behind the Earth, on the other side. So what?"

Blue leaned across in front of the pilot and adjusted a knob on an electronic screen. "We headin' away from it?"

"We better be," Hedge replied.

Blue laughed nervously, looked back at the book on his lap, and made an adjustment to the electronic screen. "Hey, yeah, see it?" he crowed.

Stel crowded the backrest to get a look at the pictograph. "Is that the way it really looks?" she asked in an awed tone.

"Yeah," Hedge said. "That's the Earth and the Moon. That little streak there must be us."

"That's us, all right," Blue assured him. "It shows our relative relationship to the Earth-Moon field of attraction. Can you read the range markings there, Hedge? I mean, on our position?"

The pilot leaned closer to the pictograph. "It looks like .012."

Blue consulted the manual again, made another adjustment to the electronic screen, and pushed a button on the nav-comm panel. An electronic hum greeted them from behind the panel. Blue looked at Tom Cole, then back to the manual. He giggled in nervous relief. "Oh, that just turned it on," he said.

"Well at least we got it turned on," Hedge commented sarcastically.

"Attention, attention, emergency broadcast," announced a robot-voice from the panel.

"I'd say we have a small emergency of our own," Stel wise-cracked. "Here we are in the depths of space, and we just learned how to turn the radio on."

Tom Cole shot the girl an irritated glance and said, "Listen!"

" . . . Gunner Zachary Whaleman, Solan emergency, repeat, Solan emergency, report to your gunship soonest possible. All charges are deferred in interests of Solan defense, repeating, all charges are deferred. Report to your . . . "

"Now just what the Mars does that mean?" Cole yelped.

Stel said, "I knew there was a—"

Hedge broke in with, "Now where does that leave us?"

The men in the rear were shuffling about nervously. Several of them surged toward the cabin. Tom Cole roared, "Stay put, just stay put!" The raiders returned to their seats, muttering to each other in subdued tones.

" . . . warning, Gunner Whaleman. Avoid all contact with zing-gun equipped automats. An ultra-sonic recepter has been emplaced in your cerebral tissues. Repeating, hazard warning, Gunner . . ."

Tom Cole's hands had flown to his head. "So that's it!" he growled.

Stel had lost all her color. She gasped "Zach—wh-what's happened to him?"

"Don't be worrying about Zach," Hedge said. "Worry begins at home. What are we—"

"Okay, stop it!" Cole commanded. "All of you, just settle down and let's take a cool look at this thing."

"We're no worse off than we were," Blue observed.

"Blue's right," Cole said. "In fact, we're better off than we've ever been. Now look, we've got a ship, and we've very near got ourselves a gunship. We may never get another chance like this one. We've got to go on with it. Ten thousand Reevers are straining at the bit right now, just waiting for our signal. If we fail them now . . ."

"We can't turn back," Blue muttered.

"No, we can't. Stel, get ahold of yourself. You'll see your redhead again, don't worry about it. And knowing Zach, I'd say the best place to find him would be Terra 10, just like we been planning all along. If he's not there yet, he'll sure as Mars be getting there as quick as he can. What do you say, Hedge?"

The big blond nodded his head curtly. "You're the king, Tom. Whatever you say suits me fine."

Blue was again fiddling with the nav-comm. He grunted with satisfaction and leaned toward the electronic screen, adjusted a control, and said, "Well. There lie the guns of Terra 10."

A tiny blip was flashing in the extreme corner of the screen. Hedge whistled softly and said, "You sure that's her?"

"I believe Zach wrote the book," Blue replied, smiling tightly.

"That's good enough for me," said Tom Cole. "Now how do we get there?"

Hedge was leaning forward to read the range markings on the screen. He yelped softly and bent closer.

"What is it?" Blue asked.

"What does 997 mean?"

"No point?" Blue was scanning a list of figures in the manual.

"No point," Hedge confirmed.

Blue whistled loudly and turned startled eyes to Tom Cole. "How many miles is in a light-minute?" he asked, awed.

"You mean a light-year?" Cole replied.

"No, I mean a light-minute." Blue pursed his lips thoughtfully and rolled his eyes toward Hedge. "186,000 miles to a second, times 60 gives you a minute."

"That's more'n ten million miles," Hedge said.

"Okay. 997, no point, means practically one light-minute. That's how far away Terra 10 is."

"That isn't possible!" Cole yelled.

"That's what it means anyway," Blue insisted.

"And it's still moving," Hedge reported, " . . . toward Venus."

"This is crazy," Stel said. "Let's go back."

"We're not going back!" Cole roared. "Hedge—will this machine take us out there?"

"I guess there's only one way to find out," Hedge replied. He turned nervous eyes to Blue. "Is everything meshed?"

"This is crazy!" Stel repeated.

Blue had soberly nodded his head in response to Hedge's query and turned to look at Tom Cole.

Cole released a noisy sigh and said, "Let's go."

Hedge's hand moved to the little box at his knee. His thumb found the button and depressed it. A low, throbbing hum issued from somewhere behind the control panel. Hedge dropped both hands to his lap, eyes glued to the accelerometer. "And away we go," he breathed. "Warp speed, coming up."

Stel's face was pressed to the viewport. A blue-green ball, far below, was rapidly diminishing in size. "Goodbye, Earth," she sighed.

CHAPTER SEVENTEEN

To Save a Ship

Whaleman had intercepted the same emergency broadcast which had been heard in the Reevers craft. He agonized for long moments over a course of action, then reluctantly inspected the communications capability of his tiny ship. The communications were minimal. He punched in on the standard Defense channel and received a responding beeptone from Moonbase.

"Gunner Whaleman," he announced into the radio, "in Space-jeep Deimos 3. Request relay channel to Terra 10."

"Standby," came the automated response. Whaleman waited several seconds, then the robot reported, "Open-intercept order from Board Island, Gunner. Standby for switchover."

Whaleman muttered, "Skronk," strongly suspecting the motives of the open-intercept.

Ian Johns-Fielding's muted excitement came in then. "Gunner Whaleman, thank God! Are you spaceborne?"

"Affirm," Whaleman replied. "And seeking Terra 10."

"Your gunship is in a runaway trajectory, Zach," the Director reported, in rising excitement. "We've tried every recycle in the book and nothing works!"

"Who is commanding?"

"Mostly automated, Zach. Sub-Gunner Rosslin is aboard but can't seem to understand the problem."

Zach grunted understandingly. Rosslin was a mere fledgling, and not too promising a one at that. "Explain situation," he snapped.

"The ferry squadron boosted her into station velocity, then withdrew. When she achieved station, she just blew right on through. She's been in runaway mode for, uh, sixteen minutes now and showing no signs of coming about. She's in the, uh, Earth-Venus maxi-corridor and closing fast on Venus."

"Sub-system alert order?"

"Yes, several times. No success. Zach—Squadroneer Bond-Durant is here with me. He says we have only minutes before impact on Venus!"

"Switch me to Luna Control," Whaleman demanded.

"Right—but I'm staying on."

A tone-note sounded, and the Terra 10 control automat on the Moon announced, "Controller."

"State Terra 10 situation," Whaleman enunciated.

There were times, Whaleman was certain, when robots exhibited near-human personalities. He could feel the surge of energy through the logic banks as the automat responded to his voice. "Situation emergency," it clipped. "Inertial runaway, negative response to control commands."

"Report subsystems status," the Gunner commanded.

The automat began feeding him digital values for each subsystem of the gunship's control features. Whaleman made no attempt to retain those which appeared nominal. The status of the stabilization-propulsion interrogation system interested him, but he allowed the automat to run through all of the suspect systems without interruption, then he ordered, "Interrogate stab-prop velocity cell."

"Skronk," responded the robot, "standby . . . reporting—stab-prop velocity responds negative, negative."

"Interrogate stab-prop grav-grab cell."

"Skronk, standby . . . reporting . . . grav-grab positive, positive. Glitch, repeat, glitch."

"Skronk," the Gunner replied. "Initiate laser penetration. Another. Initiate course vector positive swing wobble . . . five degree and swinging. Hold and report."

"Skronk. Laser penetration initiated, stab-prop subsystem. Course wobble initiated, five degree and swinging. Standby."

Whaleman stood by, ticking off the seconds in his mind. At the count of ten, the robot returned to the air with, "Positive, positive, Course alteration, five degrees and swinging. Laser penetration reports negative, negative."

"Hold wobble swing to unobstructed course, then release," Whaleman clipped back. "Continue laser penetration at 30 second intervals until positive response. Skronkback and secure."

Whaleman's own voice began returning to him, repeating his closing instructions. The robot toned off. Johns-Fielding toned in. "Is that going to fix it, Zach?" he asked breathlessly.

"Is fix impact on Venus," Whaleman replied coldly. "Terra 10 is now swinging to passing course."

"Thank God!"

"Is no time thank God. Terra 10 remains runaway mode. Laser ream-through could fix glitch, could also not. Request speak Bond-Durant."

The Squadroneer's voice bounced back. "Superior, Zach, much superior. Estimate probability control gunship."

"Probability fifty-fifty," Whaleman replied. "Contact Sub-Gunner Rosslin, update and instruct re glitch grav-grab. Synchronize manual initiation with laser penetration, interrogation circuit. Interrogation response is false, repeat false. Recycle manual to grav-grab negative, repeat negative, continuing until proper response noted."

"Skronk. Meanwhile, where is Gunner Whaleman?"

"Gunner Whaleman is in Deimos 3, spacejeep, closing on Terra 10 in maxi-corridor with all speed."

"Skronk, Zach. And . . . gratitude."

"Give also Zach's gratitude to Chairman, for addition to brain."

"I did not know of this, Zach, until too late. Skronk this, Gunner, changes are in order."

"Skronk, Squadroneer, plus changes you do not yet know."

"Do nothing foolish, Zach. Command is with you solid. Repeating, changes are in order."

"Skronk," Whaleman replied. "Tone off. I space blind, need full attention."

An override of excited voices tumbled in, then Johns-Fielding's perturbed tones cried, "Zach, the aliens are reported beyond Andro Two in the Solan Corridor!"

"What is this aliens?"

"Oh, damn, I forgot you didn't . . . "

Bond-Durant's machinelike voice recaptured the airwaves. "You can be briefed once you gain Terra 10, Zach." His words bristled with constrained emotion. "But, listen, get that gunship, and get it under control. Your guns are needed. Solana is under invasion."

Whaleman snapped, "Skronk," and turned off his communicator, then tensed at the console as the spacemonitor indicated an object overtaking him at warp speed. His deepspace companion flashed on by at near-collision proximity and quickly receded in the spacemonitor. The experience brought to Whaleman's mind the words of an ancient poet, something about "ships passing in the night." He did not wonder about the occupants of the "passing ship," but only regretted that he was not aboard his own gravcar, which could travel that fast.

He turned his mind to the "invasion" of Solana and wondered if it were really true. He had come to suspect everything issuing from Board Island. Invasion by "*aliens*?" Whaleman grinned. They had probably learned of the Reever revolt. Then he froze. The Terra 10 glitch! Was this a Reever glitch?

He fumed at the slow speed of the spacejeep and tried to focus-in his navigator. Nothing yet, no tifusion planet in runaway mode lining into his attraction focii, no wobbling sphere with ... He snapped to attention, listening to the whispering of an inner voice. *Of course, of course, perhaps he could effectively increase his speed with a bit of space-vectoring.* He reached for the communicator, received his tone, and clipped, "Luna Control, quickswitch to Terra 10 Controller ... Gunner Whaleman, Deimos 3, spacevector request, plot pursuit course to Terra 10 from these ... "

He would regain Terra 10 ... if she were regainable. He wondered if Stel, and Tom and the others were aboard ... and fervently hoped that they were not. They could be riding her right into the sun.

CHAPTER EIGHTEEN

Home is the Gunner

"Great rolling Mars!" Tom Cole exclaimed. "Isn't that a planet dead ahead?"

"That's Venus, Tom," Hedge said, his lips tight with tension.

"We're heading right into 'er!"

"No, not now. We're swinging gradually to the—See? We're going to miss."

Blue loosed a sibilant sigh. "This's the stuff nightmares are made of. I'm getting the idea we got no business out here."

Stel leaned forward and said, "Look at your speed thing, Hedge. We're slowing."

Hedge muttered, "Yes, we're down to—"

"There she is!" Cole cried. "Dead ahead! Lookit that! Isn't she a beauty?"

Blue broke the silence. He glanced at the navigation screen and said, "She's still moving, Hedge, and pretty fast. But we're overtaking."

The pilot nodded his head in agreement. "Something's going on in this stunt box under my seat. I think we're getting ready to go in."

Stel whispered, "Something's wrong with Terra 10. Can anyone else see it? It's sort of . . . wobbling."

"Something's wrong all right," Tom Cole agreed in a strained voice. "You can see it now, clear as sunlight. It's like she's . . . pulling with all she's got against Venus."

An amber light on the control panel began pulsing. Blue said, "Uh—oh, that's it. We'll be docking in about a minute."

"At *this* speed?" Hedge cried, aghast.

"Gotta figure relative speed," Blue grunted. "We're not moving much faster than Terra 10."

"What happens if we *wibble* while she *wobbles*?" Stel wondered aloud.

Blue chuckled nervously. "You gotta have faith in some things, Stel."

The gunship was filling the entire forward viewport now. Hedge reported, "Range, 100 miles and closing fast."

A man in back jerked upright, his head swivelled to the quarter viewport. "There's a meteor or something, off to the right, coming right at us."

Blue bent forward to scrutinize the navscreen. "It's a small ship," he announced. "It's, uh, yeah . . . it's heading for Terra 10, too."

Tom Cole was twisted about in his seat, glaring through the port at the approaching vehicle. "Looks like he's trying to head us off," he growled.

"Nothing's going to head us off now," Hedge grunted.

A large bay was opening in the side of Terra 10, and the gravcar was nosing into it.

"Ten seconds," Blue murmured.

"Get ready for a fight," Cole rumbled, still gazing to the rear. "That other ship's coming right in on our tail."

They moved slowly into the yawning mouth of Terra 10, though their speed indicator was still registering something better than 16,000 miles per second.

"It's like catching a moonbeam," Stel commented with a shivery sigh, and then they were settling gently into the locking mechanism of the upper dock.

"We're here," Blue declared, as though totally surprised by their success.

"We're nowhere," Stel corrected him, in subdued tones. "Babes in endless black space."

Whaleman had succeeded in switching-over the Terra 10 Communicator to a commchannel available to the spacejeep and had been in direct contact with the gunship for some minutes. He was homing-in via a makeshift radionavigation procedure and was within closing range when he noticed the other vehicle also closing on Terra 10. Now, quick to suspect villainy by Board Island, he lost no time in interrogating the gunship regarding the other craft.

"Report identity of space vehicle now in docking lane," he commanded.

The robot communicator responded with, "Vehicle is on robot homing pilot, interrogator response positive, permission to come aboard positive, automated systems positive, identity code 101 checks positive, docking procedures initiated."

"Skronk," Whaleman replied. "Maintain positive and hold for Deimos 3 like same."

"Skronk."

Whaleman did not know whether to laugh or to weep. The identity code was that of his own gravcar, which he had last seen in the possession of Tom Cole's Reevers. In Whaleman's mind, the chances of the Reevers' ever locating Terra 10, even with the gunship in Earth-orbit, were marginal at best. That they could have succeeded in tracking the runaway gunship in an inter-planetary trek was almost inconceivable. In his thinking relating the Reevers to Terra 10, his greatest fear had been that they had managed to board the gunship while she was still hovering above Board Island. The luckiest possible, in Whaleman's thinking, was that they had aborted the plan and returned to Terra.

The presence of that gravcar, now, in the Terra 10 docking lane, was most disturbing to the Gunner. Was the car occupied by Reevers? This did not seem likely. If not, then only one explanation did seem likely. The Chairman's special henchmen had captured Tom Cole and recovered the gravcar and were now boarding Terra 10 for the purpose of taking Zach Whaleman. The Gunner's mind reeled with the implications. Had he been a total idiot, a typical Reever in the classical sense, gullible to the point of stupidity? Had he fallen for a "Solan emergency" ruse to play right into the treacherous hands of the Chairman?

Precious little time remained to debate the question. He was piloting manual, and the time had arrived to line into the docking slot. He watched the other vehicle nose into the gunship's bay and knew that his decision had already been made. Whatever else, Terra 10 was definitely in jeopardy. He had to go aboard.

He moved his lips against the communicator panel and announced, "Deimos 3, now docking manual, alert receivers."

"Receivers positive," came the automated response. "Upper dock, station two, is receiving. Station one is receiving one-oh-one craft."

"Skronk," Whaleman said. "Control transfer on *three.* Initiate . . . one . . . two . . . *three.*"

"Station two control is positive, positive. Welcome home, Gunner Whaleman."

Whaleman grinned mirthlessly. Those robots *did* have a personality. Indeed, he did feel that he had returned home, Earth and all her charms notwithstanding.

CHAPTER NINETEEN

Whaleman's World

The reunion aboard Terra 10 was jubilant, boisterous, and wildly emotional. The egress lights were flashed for both craft simultaneously, the delay being governed by repressurization-time for the vehicle bay, and the Gunner of Terra 10 erupted onto the catwalk at the same instant as the Reever raiders stepped cautiously from their craft. With red-maned head cocked belligerently, and the tiny Z-gun raised and ready, Whaleman hurled his challenge a split-second before recognizing the other group.

"Hold and identify!" he cried.

"It's Zach!" yelled a ludicrously squat man in a miniature Defense Command uniform.

Tom Cole let out a whoop and launched himself along the catwalk just as a golden goddess in pleasingly distorted DefCom blue-and-black stepped out behind him. She cried, "Zach! Oh, God, *Zach*!" and led the others in the pell mell reunification.

Tears flowed unashamedly and bruises were traded ungrudgingly in the emotional jostling, grabbing, shoving and embracing that followed.

Stel was forced to fend for herself, clinging grimly to Whaleman's waist as others crushed her in wild group-embraces, and all were attempting to speak at once in the emotional release of the moment.

When the energies were spent and the emotions subsided, Stel and Zach found their ways to each other's lips, and the others stood by with self-conscious grins. And then they were trooping along in doubles along the corridor to the interior of their tifusion world, the lovers in the lead, arm-in-arm, and Zach was telling her, "Confusions are gone, Stel. I know who I am and what is my destiny." He grinned and corrected himself, "*Our* destiny."

"I've never been more frightened in my life," she admitted. "*My* confusions have only begun. All I know is that I'm with you, and it's the only thing that really matters."

"Stel will be with Zach forever," he assured her. "Yes, this is major matter." He brushed her cheek with his lips and craned back to look at Tom Cole. "Terra 10 is in glitch, Tom. Runaway mode."

"You telling me," Cole rumbled. He smiled. "We been chasing the devil all over the heavens."

"Yes, this was superior chase," Whaleman replied. "Let none now say a Reever is idiot."

"I guess the machine did it all," Cole admitted ruefully. "Gotta give credit where it's due."

"Machine does not program itself," the Gunner told him. "Is needed, human guidance. Also Terra 10 does not program herself. Board Island is discover this truth. Have you monitored this Solan emergency? This alien invasion?"

Cole said, "I've heard nothing about any alien invasion. As for the Solan emergency, it seems we've been having two or three a week for as long as I can remember. Your boys sure love to cry wolf. I gave up worrying about it a long time ago."

The party had entered a lofted area below a number of gun emplacements. Blue, hurrying along at Tom Cole's side, raised his head and whistled softly. "What's all that up there, Zach?" he asked in an awed voice.

"Up there is AGRAD Batteries 2, 4, 6, 8. Four guns, Blue."

"Just how good are those guns?" asked Hedge, peering at Whaleman between Cole and Blue.

"Enough good," Whaleman replied soberly. He twisted back to smile at Hedge. "Enough to boob Board Island into sea, Hedge."

"Damn, I'll buy that, buddy," Hedge said.

"Four of those guns could do that?" Cole asked. "How many AGRADs you got, Zach?"

"AGRADs total twenty eight. These are secondary batteries, Tom. Also twelve MAMEs, paired two to battery, effectively six guns. But one *MAME*, Tom Cole, has destructive power of all AGRADs combined."

"You could take on the solar system," Blue commented.

"Yes, plus others."

They passed through an arched doorway and onto a gently curving ramp. Zach squeezed Stel's hand and said, "This rises to Command Cabin. Is nice. Stel will like."

Blue was still thinking about the guns. He scampered along, laboring to meet the long strides of his companions, and huffed, "Zach . . . where do you get all the energy for these guns? Isn't there an ultimate limit?"

Whaleman nodded his head. "Yes, Blue, ultimate limit is energy radiation of Sol."

"Huh?"

"Correction, of all galactic Sols. Heart of Terra 10 is magnetherm core. Is constantly replenished by captured gamma radiation, X-radiation, plus others. Terra 10 is perpetual energy machine."

"It's more than that," Hedge said. "There's a very definite *up* and *down* here. You have an artificial gravity."

"Is not artificial, Hedge. Is another feature of magnetherm core, plus supporting systems. Terra 10 is miniature earth. Has north pole, south pole, complete gravitational field. *Down* as you say, is core attraction. *Up* is reverse, toward surface."

''We saw the thing wobbling as we approached,'' Stel said. ''What made it stop?''

Whaleman grinned. ''Is not stop, wobble continues.''

''Then why can't we feel it?''

''Does Stel feel Earth wobble? Earth also wobbles, Stel. Gunship in runaway mode. Earlier, danger was that gunship would impact Venus. We introduce variation to magnetic field, cause wobble, change course, gunship does not impact Venus.''

''Then this thing really is in trouble,'' Tom Cole commented.

''Yes, Tom, is serious glitch. First, we must conquer Terra 10.'' He turned and smiled. ''Second, we conquer ourselves. Third, we conquer Board Island.''

Cole was scowling, in deep thought. Hedge said, ''I'll buy that.''

Whaleman pulled the group to a halt at the top of the ramp, directed them onto a motorized stairway, then waved his hand in front of a photoelectric cell which was mounted on the bulkhead. The stairway began moving and a heavy hatch at the top swung open. ''This is Whaleman's World,'' he declared proudly, swinging an arm across the void beyond the stairway.

''Whaleman's World'' was a technological wonderland of automated consoles by the score, light panels, monitor stations, relay boards, power stations, clicking circuits, and whirring computers, stretching in a seeming infinity through the interior well of Terra 10 in a bewildering array. He halted the stairway momentarily at the midpoint so that all could have a look.

Following a brief, awed silence, Stel said, ''You run all this, Zach? One man? By yourself?''

''Yes, Stel, one man . . . but many machines.

Terra 10 is a machine, run by many sub-machines, all reporting ultimately to the Gunner. Submachines are brains of Terra 10, but the Gunner is the mind. This is important, never forget, only man has the mind."

He started the stairway again and they went on through the open hatch and into the command cabin. It was spacious, but not to the point of comfortably accommodating so many visitors. A master console occupied a dais at the center. Various other pedestal-type consoles were scattered about, and the walls of the turret-like room were completely covered with panels, light indicators and viewscreens. A clear-dome ceiling projected beyond the surface of the gunship, apparently protruding at a sharp angle. "Observatory," Whaleman explained, pointing to the dome.

A very tall female came to her feet and stared silently at them from the master console. She appeared to be of about Whaleman's general height, somewhat slighter of build and more rounded in critical places, shiny black hair cropped close in a boyish fashion with full sideburns and tight curls across the forehead. She wore the blue and black of the Defense Command and held herself in a stiffly military posture. Stel nudged Whaleman with an elbow. As he turned into full view, the girl at the console inclined her head in the formal salute and said, "Ho, Gunner."

Whaleman returned the salute and raised a hand in greeting, then wordlessly led his group to the console. He thrust Stel to the forefront. "Sub-Gunner Rosslin, this is Stel Rogers/Brandt." He also introduced Tom Cole and each of the raiders in turn. The girl stared with frank interest at their uniforms, especially those adorning Blue and several other Homan-sized men, and her eyes kept returning to the projections at Stel's chest.

Whaleman's only explanation was, "These have accompanied me from Terra. Primary task is to correct control glitch. Report status, Sub-Gunner."

The girl's voice was cool and crisp. "Status remains unchanged, Gunner. Instructions relayed via DDC have been followed, results negative." She crumbled a bit then and raised a trembling hand to her forehead. "Gunner . . . DDO advises that Gunner Whaleman re-assumes command Terra 10. Rosslin happily relinquishes. Request immediate."

Whaleman smiled and embraced her, said, "Well done, Rosslin," and moved quickly to the console. He made a cursory inspection of the indications, then raised his eyes to the girl. "Isolation shield negative?" he queried.

She nodded. "Negative, all recycles. Plus, maneuvering subsystems all negative. Solid glitch, all controls."

Whaleman nodded his head and murmured something beneath his breath, as though talking to the console. Then he said, "Rosslin, take guests to command billet. Rest, make friends, eat, refresh."

The girl replied, "Skronk," and turned her gaze to Tom Cole. He grinned at her and let his eyes travel her frame. Her eyes fled the confrontation and she murmured, "Tom Cole is no Commander."

"Bet on that," he said, enunciating carefully. "But, aren't there better things?"

She pushed on past him and said, "Please follow."

Whaleman met the Reever chief's questioning gaze and nodded his head in reassurance. "Stel, too, follow," he said, smiling at her. "Zach much busy, immediate time next."

"Don't dehumanize, Zach," she said plaintively.

His smile broadened. "Not this Reever," he assured her.

She went over and kissed him, then followed the others out of the cabin. Zach waited until the hatch closed, then he began rapidly positioning switches, setting up alternate command circuits. "Now, my friends," he whispered, "talk to Zach."

"DDO from Terra 10. Gunner Whaleman reporting status."

"Go ahead, Zach. Squadroneer Bond-Durant here."

"Circuit fusion, command logic. Reroute, alternate circuits using gunnery logic, has bypassed glitch. Control is now positive. Using trajectory swing to come around on Terra. Velocity sixteen-two-eighty per second, range from Terra two-five-point-eight million. Request defense assignment."

A pause, then, "Skronk, Zach. Does this mean batteries cannot be activated?"

"Affirmative. Gunnery logic substituting for command logic."

"Skronk. If able attain defense station, can logic be restored to primary batteries?"

"Only if ferry squadron can take gunship in tow. Unable maintain station with negative control."

Another pause, then, "Zach, every ship in command is ordered to defense slot at outer envelope. This is massive invasion. Estimated two full flotillas, plus more still following in outer corridor."

"Skronk. So, no ferry squadron."

"Problem is, Zach, time factor. Unable return ships plus station gunship in effective time. Suggestions?"

"Squadroneer, this glitch is no glitch. This glitch is sabotage."

"Unskronk. Explain."

"Cause of control circuit fusion is outside

source. Interrogate intelligence computer, ascertain probability that outside source is alien ships."

"Zach, this is . . . Skronk. Standby."

"Standing by. Plus, altering course, proceeding Solan corridor."

"No time, Zach, no time. DDO suggests Terra 10 attempt achieve gravity-orbit earth-moon system, disable bypass control features, activate batteries for all possible defense Mother Planet."

"Negative, negative, this is ineffective procedure. Dead orbit neutralizes defense capability, aggressors can attack at will on blind side of orbit."

"Bitter truth, Zach, Terra 10 is not ultimate defense. In such case, is no defense at all. Planning glitch, Zach."

"Negative, Terra 10 will perform defense assignment. Reporting course change positive, velocity same, proceeding Solan corridor."

"Problem is simple mathematics, Zach. If alien fleet passes defense perimeter, Terra will be gone long before Terra 10 achieves Solan corridor. Standby, intelligence computer report. Is positive, Zach. Probability is seventy-thirty positive."

"Skronk, this checks my data. Automated report follows."

"Hold, Zach. Words from Chairman."

"Chairman can save . . . apology, Terra 10 standing by for Chairman."

The precise tones of the Chairman's automat came through. "Chairman requests probability of Terra 10 achieving Solan corridor for effective defense posture."

Whaleman said, "Terra 10 standing by for Chairman, not for Chairman's automat."

A pause, then the reedy voice, "Gunner, are you in full possession of your senses?"

"Affirmative."

"Your insistence upon proceeding to the solar

corridor smacks of sheer emotionalism. Your defense station has been assigned. You are to proceed without delay to a gravity-orbit of Earth, where you will then place your batteries in the automatic-ready mode."

"Negative."

"You are directly disobeying a Command decision?"

"Affirmative. Chairman has proved to be fallible. Many errors noted. Terra 10 will make Command decisions. Recommend Chairman interrogate intelligence computer re: probability aliens monitoring all Solana communications. This should check positive, repeat positive. Terra 10 will transmit automated data, then go comm-dead, repeat comm-dead. Zach off."

Whaleman deactivated the communications console and swung about to regard Sub-Gunner Rosslin with a steady gaze. "So," he told her, "umbilical is severed."

Her eyes dropped. "Eva Rosslin serves the Commander of Terra 10," she murmured. Her gaze came back up, swung to the group of Reevers who were conversing among themselves in the doorway, then returned to Whaleman. "But what are these? This Tom Cole is no Commander."

"This Tom Cole is a Reever," Whaleman told her.

Her eyes flared noticeably. "And this female with motherhood chest, this also is Reever, plus all?"

Whaleman nodded. "Plus Zach Whaleman."

The girl sank weakly into a command chair. "Is nightmare," she said.

"No, is awakening *from* nightmare. Does Rosslin still serve Commander of Terra 10?"

"What else?" she asked dully.

The Gunner flipped a lever, bringing a viewscreen to life, then sharpened the focus. "Observe, solar corridor."

The girl straightened and stared at the screen. "Many cruisers," she commented.

"Yes, plus others, top of barrel." He raised to his full height and signalled to the group in the doorway.

The Reevers approached the command console and arranged themselves in a fan behind it. Two of the men had removed their uniforms and wore only crotchguards. Whaleman swept them with a disapproving glance and said, "Get in uniform."

"What for, Zach?" replied one. "You said get comfortable."

Whaleman waved a hand in front of him, like a high priest conferring a benediction. "Gunner of Terra 10 commissions these men, this woman, in name of Solana." He grinned. "These Reevers are now Defense Commanders." He glared at the two unclothed ones. "Get in uniform!"

The two men laughed and trotted quickly out of the cabin. "And report back soonest!" Whaleman called after them.

Tom Cole was giving Whaleman a curious stare. "What's going on here, Zach?" he asked testily.

The Gunner pointed to the viewscreen. "There is your cry wolf, Tom Cole. Emergency is real."

The big Reever chieftain was peering into the viewscreen with a perplexed expression. "Where is this?" he asked.

"Solan corridor to Andro. This is also called *Galactic Slot.*" He leaned forward and traced a circle with his finger around a clump of lights near the top of the screen. "This is alien ships. You see many."

"Maybe they're friendly," Stel suggested.

Whaleman shook his head. "Too many for friendly. Plus, combat formations. Plus, intelligence computer reports no life signs from ships, but heavily armed. No, Stel, this is invasion fleet."

"How can you know all this?" Cole asked, his voice hotly irritated.

Whaleman shrugged. "Is just know, Tom. Is irrefutable data."

"Well I don't buy your damn irrefutable data," Cole snarled. "Those zingoes down there on Board Island are pulling a ringer on us. This is the first chance the Reevers have had in centuries, and I'm not gonna throw it away."

Whaleman brought a balled fist from deep space and sent it crashing into Tom Cole's unprepared face. The big fellow staggered backwards, hit the wall, and slid to a sitting position on the deck. He shook his head viciously, tried to get up, and fell over onto his outstretched hands. Sub-Gunner Rosslin sat frozen to her chair, staring at Whaleman in bewilderment. Tom Cole rose to one knee, then took the girl's hand and merely held it.

Whaleman said, "Tom hits Zach, wake Zach up. Now Zach hits Tom. Is Tom woke up?"

The big Reever chuckled, rubbed his chin, and came to his feet. "Okay, Zach," he said amiably, "you're right. What's in your mind?"

"Reever's freedom to live is worth fight," the Gunner told him. "Freedom to die, no. First assignment, Tom, is save some place for Reevers to live. Next, win freedom. Skronk?"

"Skronk," Cole replied, grinning. "How much of a fight is this going to be, Zach?"

Whaleman looked back to the screen. "Is seem Defense Command have superiority, many more ships than invaders. Not so. More ships, yes, but many are unfit to fight. No good, Tom. Defense Cruisers will not hold invaders. Terra 10 is needed."

"So what do we do? Is this thing still out of control?"

Whaleman quickly briefed his "crew" on the status of Terra 10. He completed the assessment with, "So, this is problem. Plus mathematical one. How get Terra 10 to Solan corridor in time?"

"Well what's pushing us right now?" Cole asked. "Isn't there some way to just speed it up?"

"No, Tom. Push is basic law of motion, inertia. Terra 10 is prop-dead, meaning no propulsion plant, except for minor maneuvers using gravitational system."

Tom Cole threw up his hands. "So, Mars, buddy, you've got a problem here that can't be solved."

Whaleman's gaze fell on Blue. "Reevers can steal gravcar, leave Terra first time, find way to moving speck near Venus. This is human mind, in all its excellence. Can human mind push Terra 10 to combat?"

"It was your machine, Zach," Blue muttered. "We just followed the instructions and pushed the buttons."

"Did *mind* push buttons, Blue?"

The small Reever stared at his hands, then took a deep breath and said, "You got this isolation shield. You got a gravitational system, and you *say* the energy potential of the universe. There oughta be some way to put it all together."

The Gunner was grinning like a happy Reever. "We make gravcar of Terra 10?" he said.

Hedge cried, "Hey, you just might have something there!"

"You're way over my head," Tom Cole rumbled.

"Me too," piped in Stel. "But I'll sing songs and wash the dishes, if that'll help any."

A small, dark, intent youth edged forward, peering at the Gunner shyly. He swallowed hard and said, "If this is Whaleman's World, then I guess you can do anything you want to with it, Zach. You tell me what to do, and I'll do it."

Whaleman's eyes moistened. He said, in barely audible tones, "Guns of Terra 10 will speak for man. They will speak in the Solan corridor."

None present doubted the truth of that statement.

CHAPTER TWENTY

Talking Guns

Whaleman dispatched Eva Rosslin and most of his new crew into the interior maze of Terra 10. The Sub-Gunner's task was to set up a fire-control communications network between the various batteries, to station a "gunman" at each battery and to instruct each gunman in the simple procedures of firing the guns in the local-control mode.

Remaining in the Command Cabin with Whaleman were Stel, Blue, and Hedge. Tom Cole was double-teaming with Eva Rosslin and "getting the feel" of the gunship.

Whaleman was explaining warp-speed concepts to his companions. "Is warp, meaning *distortion*. Is like, shortest distance between two points is straight line, but in space, all straight lines are, believe this, distorted lines."

"How can they be straight and warped at the same time?" Hedge asked.

"Apology, Hedge, is in appearance. Understand, space has dimensions not detectable by human senses. Open space appears straight. Is not. Is curved. Apparent straight line through apparent straight space is actually *curved* line. Like same on earth, any sphere."

"You mean," Blue commented, "the straight line from America to Asia is right through the earth, not curved across the surface."

"This is like same," Whaleman agreed. "Surface of sphere, if sphere large enough, appears straight . . . flat. Like early man, thought Earth was flat. Not flat. Curved. Space not flat. Space also curved. Flat space is illusion, like flat Earth. Flat space illusion is created by physical properties of space, not detectable by human senses. This caused early confusions in science. Early science was like so: Observe, report, make conclusions. Conclusions made were based on observations. Early scientists observed that light always travels in straight line."

"Yeah," Blue said, "and they also decided that the speed of light is the ultimate speed limit in the universe."

"Yes, and this is true in three-dimensional space. But space has more than three dimensions. Error was caused by fact that light diffuses only in three dimensions. Human observation limited by dimensions into which light diffuses, or travels. Light does not burrow below third dimension, but diffuses evenly along apparent flat space."

"Hey, you're talking like a tunnel, aren't you," Hedge said, seeing a glimmer. "It's like a mountain that's a mile up and a mile down. A path over the mountain, from one side to the other, would be two miles long. Maybe the damn mountain is only half a mile thick. Dig a tunnel through, and you're only going half a mile instead of two miles."

"Yes, Hedge, this is like same. And now, assume that you could run at speed of light, either over mountain or—"

"Damn—damn!" Blue exclaimed. "That explains faster-than-light. FTL is only an apparent value."

"Right, this is right! Is relativity value. Speed of object is measured as time consumed between two points. Right?"

"Right, *damn* right," Blue said, highly enthused. "Okay, I got that picture, Zach. Now . . . you're saying that a warp-speed is just tunneling through curved space instead of riding the curves. I got that."

"Me, too, I guess," Hedge muttered. "But . . . how do you get into the warp? I mean . . . "

"Aha!" Whaleman said, obviously delighted with his pupils. "Now we arrive at what Tom Cole calls 'the nutty butty.' How to find *real* straight line through space. Recall earlier discussion of isolation shield? Zach explains energy repulsion within atom? This repulsion is caused by unobservable property of atom, is *deeper dimension* of atom, all atoms, everywhere. This deeper dimension is *buffer*, separates matter of atom from anti-matter of atom. Skronk?"

"I think so," said Blue. "Go on."

"This buffer is *corridor*, straight through atom."

"Yeah?"

"Is yeah. Solar system is *giant* atom, Hedge. Is have like same properties of atom, is have corridors also. Plus, corridors separate different solar systems, also galaxies. Universe is like giant Swiss cheese, is have corridors run everywhere." He tapped the viewscreen. "Here is corridor, Andro to Solana. Here is where guns of Terra 10 must talk."

"This is spooky," Stel breathed.

"How does a gravcar find the warp," Blue asked solemnly.

"Gravcar creates warp, falls through."

"All right, how does it *create* the warp?"

"This involves complicated physics, Blue, no time now to fully explain. Involves mass contraction of moving object, speed distortion of three-dimensional space. Gravity field of gravcar retards contraction although great three-dimension speed is attained. Result is that space surrounding gravcar suffers much greater distortion than does gravcar. Gravcar then enters first parallel corridor to open. This is principle."

"I'd like to learn more about it when we get more time."

"You will," Zach assured him. He glanced

again at the viewscreen. "For now, let us 'put it all together,' as you say. Let us give Terra 10 a grav drive that achieves warp speed."

"I'm game," Hedge said. "How do we go about it?"

"Go about first removing shielding from magnetherm core, one full quadrant. Then—"

"Is that dangerous?"

"Could be, precautions are possible. Then go about mating core to maneuvering system. Then go about mating isolation system to this, except isolation is reversed. Then go about altering isolation system for beam transmission instead of multi-directional broadcast. Then, maybe, Terra 10 is a gravcar."

"God, it sounds like a year's work," Hedge declared.

"We have, at most, one Terran hour."

"Then I hope to God you know what you're doing."

"Zach hopes to God also." He rose quickly to his feet. "Come, we invade the machines."

In a matter of some fifty Terran minutes, a near-miracle of technology was produced by Zach Whaleman and his Reever assistants. The gunship Terra 10, designed only to function as a barely mobile space station, was transformed to a space greyhound, an inter-galactic dreadnaught capable of ranging farther and faster than man had ever dared dream. All this, however, was not immediately evident, not even to the minds which had conceived and engineered the triumph.

Zach Whaleman was seated at the Command Console, Hedges/Bolsom at the Core Monitor to Whaleman's right, and on the other side at the Communications Monitor was Fontainbleu/Oraskny. Stel Rogers/Brandt occupied the observatory, directly above Whaleman. Tom Cole and Sub-Gunner Rosslin shared a MAME gunport in the southern hemisphere. The interior communications net provided a personal inlet/outlet for each crewmember, allowing instantaneous transfer of information from any point to all points within the gunship.

Blue reported, without looking up from his console, "Lot of stuff coming out of that corridor, just about everything in the electromagnetic spectrum."

Whaleman snapped, "Attempt isolate and analyze anything alien."

"Skronk. I got the machine working on a couple now."

Hedge said, "Core is at optimum, Zach. How's our velocity?"

"Disappointing, Hedge. Building too slowly."

"Aren't we going to make it?"

"If warp speed not attained in thirty seconds, I will initiate tumble."

"What's that mean?" from Tom Cole.

"Rotation along plane. Equatorial spin, Tom. Like Earth."

Stel said, "You mean we're going to roll like a ball?"

"Means this. No fear, Stel. Remember, *down* is toward core, *up* is toward skin. Even tumbling, this is true. Like same on Earth."

"What'll that do?" Blue asked.

"Time is now. Tumble initiated. Now we see what does, Blue. Should soon note forcefield buildup. Forget optimum now, Hedge. Give me Scale Four output."

"Skronk. Scale Four initiated. Coming up. Mark, core is Scale Four."

"Ah, ah, yes, is talking to Zach. Warp speed coming up. Stel, report plane declination."

"Minus three and depressing. Minus four . . . five . . . holding at minus five."

Whaleman spoke into an analog computer. "Decline is minus five from apparent. Report corridor effect."

"Skronk," came the whirring reply. "Standby . . . corridor effect positive, intersect solar access at one-one-three moments, net velocity FTl 2.4."

"Skronk," Whaleman replied. His fingers danced along a line of buttons, then he grinned and spoke into the communicator. "Success, Terra 10 goes to war."

"At nearly two-and-a-half times the speed of light," Blue's awed tones added.

Whaleman requested, "No speak now until solar access achieved."

"Zach's flying this thing by the seat of his pants," explained Tom Cole, quite unnecessarily.

All aboard understood the makeshift nature of their navigation system. Two computers, an analog and a digital, were hooked in tandem to the juryrigged maneuvering system, which was in turn crossed with the isolation system, providing a rather crude guidance control. But the desired effect had been achieved. The isolation field was now an attracting field, capable of being beamed with pinpoint accuracy over a virtually infinite distance. Any large stellar body could be utilized as a focal field, and the velocity of the gunship was directly related to the strength of the attraction-field, which in turn was a direct product of the energies released by the gunship's magnetherm core, which itself took its energies from the stellar fields. Whaleman had tapped and harnessed the energy potential of the universe.

"Be ready," Whaleman clipped tersely. "Moment approaching. Expect violent motion during wobble-turn, slowdown. Standby, Hedge. Give me Scale Three at mark, Scale Two at next mark, Optimum at third mark."

"Skronk."

Whaleman's hands flew along the console buttons. He said, "Mark!" The gunship lurched, then smoothly stabilized. "Mark!" Another lurch, less violent, then, "Mark!"

Terra 10 was in the solar access corridor between Sol and Andro and executing a wide, sweeping turn up the million-mile-diameter barrel.

Stel reported, "Ecliptic normal."

"I'll never be normal again," Tom Cole admitted, in a barely recognizable voice.

"There's some real odd wave energy all over the place," Blue worriedly reported. "It does not analyze."

"Switching over to inertial," Zach said. "Hedge, initiate isolation transfer. Restore core shielding. Gunmen, stand ready."

"Ships dead ahead!" Stel cried. "Swarms."

Whaleman energized the target screen. "Ours," he said quickly. "Do not fire."

The Solani cruisers were moving downstream, counter to Terra 10's movement. Whaleman punched in the inter-ship communicator just in time to receive a greeting from the flagship. "Is that Terra 10?" asked a strained human voice.

"Affirmative," Whaleman replied, "this is Reevercraft Terra 10. What is situation, Squadroneer?"

"Situation poor, Gunner. What is this Reevercraft? Unskronk."

Whaleman grinned at Hedge and replied, "New class dreadnaught, Squadroneer. Reever planned and manned. Now assuming firstline station. Request briefing."

"Mars Squadron now null, plus Venus Squadron, Mercury Squadron. This is Jupiter Squadron plus stragglers first three named. Sixteen alien craft verified destroyed plus ten possibles. We are falling back to inner perimeter for regroup. Enemy also in regroup situation, but situation poor, Gunner. Is Terra 10 in defense posture?"

"Affirmative. Terra 10 is on station and closing. This is Command. Skronk? Terra 10 assumes firstline. Squadrons will remain clear and hold at inner perimeter. Terra 10 guns are on manual-local control and human manned. Gunmen not versed in craft recognition, will fire on anything moving through defense envelope. Repeating, squadrons will remain clear, give Terra 10 firstline."

"Is this true, Gunner—Reevers manning guns of Terra 10?"

"This is true, Squadroneer."

"The squadrons will remain clear, Gunner. Solan Slot belongs to Terra 10."

Blue cried, "Zach, I don't like this wave energy!"

Whaleman promptly moved a lever on his console and announced, "Isolation shield activated."

"That did it!" Blue exulted. "Radiation reception now negative! That shield really works, Zach. I was afraid we'd messed it up, screwing it around the way we did."

The Gunner smiled. "Observe target screen. Works also on physical masses."

Two of the retreating Solani cruisers, which had been straggling past the gunship had become suddenly displaced in space, from a position only a few miles abeam Terra 10, to a new location one thousand miles distant. Hedge grinned and said, "Whuup, lookout boys, low tunnel!"

"Yes, is good example of curved space," Whaleman pointed out.

"Couldn't they warp us, Zach?" Blue asked. "I mean, these aliens, if they understand—"

"They understand," Whaleman assured him. "But isolation shield is warp-lock, is manipulate space at maximum distortion."

Stel said, "Can I come down now? Can't see a thing up here now."

Whaleman replied, "Yes, Stel, come down. All seeing now is at penetration frequency only. Gunsights, yes. Optics, no."

"It's weird," announced Tom Cole's voice. "This gunsight is like a flashlight in a dark room."

Whaleman was peering intently at the target screen. "Stand ready, gunmen," he ordered. "Solani squadrons now all clear. The slot belongs to Terra 10. Destroy all else."

"All I see is a lot of junk, debris," declared an excited voice from a distant gunport.

"We approach combat zone," Whaleman explained. "Remember, gunmen, let target center in gunsight. All targets are valid."

Stel shivered and leaned against Whaleman. "All those poor men out there . . . or whatever they are . . . beings. Maybe they have anxious women waiting for them, somewhere, wherever they came from."

"No beings," Whaleman murmured. "No women, also. Alien craft fully automated, no life forms aboard."

"We're fighting nothing but a bunch of machines, Stel," Blue said softly.

"Boobs," Whaleman said, smiling grimly. "Is natural enemy of man, is not?"

"You can say that loudly, brother Whaleman!" Tom Cole commented from his polar gunport. "And I think I'm gettin' a target. Lookit this thing here, Eva girl, and tell me what I'm gettin'."

"This is target, Tom Cole," a soft-crisp voice

replied. "Is your honor, King Tom, first shot from Terra 10. Range is . . . point eight eight million . . . hold until centerlined. Remember, we tumble."

"Gotcha. Here's a big loud word for mankind. Mars! I can feel the energy tingling my hand. Good God of all the stars! Can the rest of you *see* that bolt? Great spinning Mars—I didn't know I could speak *that* loud!"

A superagitated release of gamma rays had instantaneously found their programmed path from Tom Cole's paired batteries through the protectively warped space surrounding the gunship; from the forward wall of the defense shield, the two sizzling beams arced into the blackness of space like interstellar lightning. The beam from the *matter-emitter* was focalizing the loosely scattered particles of deepspace matter, pulling them into the attracting path of sheer energy, cannibalizing the atoms, stripping them, releasing the stored energy of the particles and adding that energy to its own content—thus, the beam fed on space itself and geometrically increased its strength as it travelled.

The companion beam from the *antimatter-emitter* performed in an identical manner, though gathering and releasing the stored energy of *anti*-particles. The paired beams annihilated space between the gunship and its target as the gamma rays streaked across the void, coming together at the point of impact upon the alien craft. When the two fantastically charged rays of incompatible energies met at the target, the great disc from another world glowed momentarily with a brilliant incandescence as its atoms trembled under the assault of nuclear reaction. As the nuclei split under the bombardment of hyperfission, the glow flashed into instant annihilation of the matter composing the craft, and the alien ship simply ceased to be.

Tom Cole released the firing button, sucked in his breath, and leaned closer into the gunsight. "Where'd it go?" he said in a hushed voice.

Subgunner Rosslin murmured, "Is spacedust, Tom."

Up in the command cabin, Blue commented, "Ashes to ashes, and dust to . . . " His words choked under a quiet emotion and he bent over his console as other guns began their monologue of destruction.

The gleaming sphere that was Terra 10 was rotating slowly on her poles and sweeping along the Solar-Andron slot at dead center, her primary batteries reaching out to ream the entire corridor along the path of advance, like a cleaning brush in a giant gun barrel. As the range closed between the opposing forces, the monologue became a dialogue as the invaders responded. Swarms of alien craft, great whirling discs in precise combat formation, were speeding along the corridor to meet the giant sphere and sending out impressive streamers of explosive energies in beams extending thousands of miles in advance. These beams did not deflect from the isolation shield of Terra 10, but seemed to react with the gunship's energy field, exploding into great towering balls of flame at the outer perimeter of the shield.

Whaleman was anxiously watching the results in his viewscreen. He began feeding data into the analog computer. Stel, standing beside him, flinched with each challenge to the gunship's shield, her eyes widely staring at the mushrooming energies building up along their forward wall. Whaleman turned to Blue and said, "Advise immediate any traces wave indications."

Blue replied, "Skronk."

Whaleman snapped, "Hedge, increase to Scale Two. Velocity diminishes!"

"Skronk. Scale Two . . . mark. What's doing it, Zach?"

Whaleman frowned worriedly. "Enemy salvos not piercing, also not deflecting. Energy masses build up. Inertial law, Hedge. Motion of moving body remains constant until impressed by opposing forces. These energies are make impressing force, like brake, like atmosphere to dense-air craft."

"AGRADs, stand ready!" Subgunner Rosslin commanded into the intercom.

Blue fidgeted and remarked, "Too many are getting past the MAMEs, Zach. Can those AGRADs handle them?"

Before the Gunner could reply to Blue's query, Hedge cried, "Scale Two isn't doing it, Zach!"

"Scale Three!"

"Skronk! Coming up on Scale Three . . . mark! But she's not steady!"

Stel murmured, "They're throwing up a wall out there. That's what they're doing. What happens if they stop us?"

"Stop not necessary," Whaleman replied worriedly.

Blue explained, "All they have to do is slow us below warp speed. Then we'll lose the corridor, and it'll be all theirs."

Stel's fingers dug into Whaleman's shoulder. "Well, let's go faster," she urged.

Whaleman shook his head. "Guns also use core energies. Core now suffers severe strain."

Tom Cole roared, "Mars, it's like going after an anthill with a hatchet! Lookit them Boobs stunting around out there!"

"Yes, Tom, Zach watches. Analog also watches. If pattern emerges, these stunts will defeat Boobs."

"Just lemme know when you figure it out!"

Hedge asked, "What's he talking about?"

Whaleman was busy with the analog computer. Stel pointed to the viewscreen. "Just watch them," she said in a hushed voice.

The enemy vehicles were apparently capable of lightning-quick lateral displacements, an entire formation disappearing from one field and reappearing instantly in a greatly displaced parallel field. It was proving to be an effective tactic; the Reever gunners were missing more than they were hitting.

Whaleman looked up from the analog and spoke into the intercom. "Rosslin, closing range now below MAME minimums, lead vehicles. Plus, enemy batteries impede Terra 10's progress. Gunnery score must improve."

The Subgunner replied, "Skronk. Secondary batteries activated."

Tom Cole's big voice filled the intercom. "You Reeves on the AGRADS, did you hear that? How many you people ever been boobed? How many of you ever had a Boob in a gunsight before? I hope to crying Mars you're not letting any of them *out* of your gunsights in one piece! Huh?"

"Are them Boobs, Tom?" asked a surprised and distant gunman.

"Same damn thing! Machines, coming over here to run us out! Right, Zach?"

"Right, is like same."

"Hey, Boob!" someone yelled.

The gunship became a riot of exultant sounds. Stel leaned low over Whaleman's shoulder and said, "They'll do better now, Zach. Now it's a holy war."

"What is this holy war?"

Blue smiled grimly. "A very old human preoccupation, Gunner. You can think of it as a *hate* war. Do you skronk *hate?*"

Whaleman nodded. "Yes, this human has learned to skronk hate."

Hedge cried, "The core's going nuts!"

Whaleman glanced at Hedge's instruments and hastily tattooed instructions into the power banks. Blue yelled, "Hey! I'm getting wave forms!"

"Analysis!" Whaleman snapped.

"Negative! They don't analyze!"

Stel warned, "Look at the tumble indicator!"

Whaleman fought with a command circuit as a mechanized voice from his console announced, "Hazard, hazard. Isolation shield breached."

Whaleman turned to Hedge and snarled, "Scale Four!"

"Skronk!"

Blue said, "Okay, I'm getting a readout now. It's a reverse sine!"

"Hazard, hazard," again announced the automat. "Fusion energies are present."

Whaleman whirled to Blue's console and briefly studied the flickering display on the wave analyzer. "Anti-energy!" he said, alarmed.

"What?" Blue cried.

"Is anti-energy wave. Is cause fusion, not like same fission. Like same, earlier sabotage of Terra 10 control circuits. Yes, this is how."

"You mean anti-matter?"

"No, mean anti-energy. Remember lesson? Energy cannot be destroyed. This is not like same, Blue. This is *anti*-energy."

"So?"

"So . . . lesson is maybe wrong. Is maybe possible, energy *is* destroyed by anti-energy. Like same, matter and anti-matter."

"God, I don't understand that!" Blue replied dismally.

A wheeling disc loomed up in the viewscreen. Stel moved instinctively, jerking back in a startled reaction to the sudden confrontation with an enemy craft at close range. An immediate salvo from several AGRAD batteries caught the challenger in a convulsive torque of opposition, the anti-gravity beams shredding through the mass of suddenly tortured metals; atomic structures lost their coalescing bonds, and the invading spacecraft began to melt and liquefy. As Stel watched in horrified fascination, the entire mass of metal pulled apart into shapeless jellylike blobs and, as deterioration progressed, into rapidly scattering vapors.

"That's h-horrible!" she gasped.

"Is diffusion," Whaleman explained. "Is AGRAD principle, is *un*-creation." He was running his fingers along a row of command buttons. "Is like opposite, this anti-energy maybe. Is maybe opposite happen to Terra 10, this anti-energy penetration." penetration."

"You mean, it'll contract us!" Blue exclaimed. "It'll freeze us into a no-energy lump of contracted matter!"

"Maybe not so!" The Gunner was extracting a readout from the analog. He gripped Stel's hand and put a beeptone on the intercom to signal for attention. Then he announced, "Ho, Gunmen. Here are your Boobs, these stunts. Here is logic, pattern. Shift is—"

Tom Cole interrupted the announcement. "They won't read you, Zach. Let me explain what you mean. Listen, Reeves. Zach has their stunts figured. You listen to what he says, then you can make them stunt right into your gunsights. That right, Zach?"

"Is right. This is pattern. Shift is starboard, two gunmarks . . . starboard, one gunmark. Next, is shift port one gunmark; port, three gunmarks; port, two gunmarks. Then repeating like same. This is pattern."

"So you boys know what to do!" Cole rumbled. "Set up a counter pattern. Bring the Boobs to your gunsights. Skronk?"

An enthusiastic *skronk* chorus rang through the intercom.

Whaleman had already returned his attention to Blue's wave analyzer. Stel moved closer to the viewscreen, which was now showing multiple targets at increasingly closer ranges. The AGRAD batteries were now sending out sizzling diffusion beams with a stark effect. The foreground of the viewscreen was becoming obscured with the clouds of vaporized vehicles. The outer range, in the upper portion of the screen, was being constantly illuminated by the brilliant flashes of long-distance MAME strikes. Instantly, an adjacent screen became illuminated, revealing scattered targets slipping past on the gunship's beams.

Rosslin's quiet tones came over the intercom. "AGRADs One, Three, Five . . . targets abeam . . . Gunner, suggest stabilize gunship . . . quadrant assignments now required."

"Skronk, affirmative!" Whaleman replied. He turned to Hedge and snapped, "Secure tumble!"

"Skronk . . . tumble secured."

"Stabilized," Blue reported.

The tumbling motion of Terra 10 was arrested, and with it, a dangerous decrease of her forward velocity.

Hedge warned, "Scale Four's not gonna hold her without that tumble."

Rosslin was instructing the gunmen. "Assume quadrant defense assignments. Odd-sector AGRADs, you have corridor-penetration targets!"

Additional target viewscreens were beginning to illuminate. Stel murmured, "A lot of them are getting through."

"Don't worry, Zach," Tom Cole's voice boomed through, "We'll mop them up. They won't get far past us!"

"Worry is wave energies," Whaleman muttered. He was punching out instructions to the digital computer. "Blue, report penetration level."

"Level 10 at the skin, and building. Level is 1,000 at the outer perimeter, so we're still keeping most of it out. What's the danger limit?"

"This is interrogation," the Gunner replied, as he fed the information into the digital. He punched the command button and turned a level gaze toward Blue, awaiting the automated report.

The robot whirred, "Tolerance level is 100 units per cubic centimeter of tifusion mass. Energy decay rate through isolation shield is at group 5 ratio."

Whaleman commented to Blue, "This is answer. Danger limit at skin is Level 25."

Stel gasped, "Look at the third screen, Zach! They've hit one of their own ships!"

A nearby hurtling disc had apparently stunted into the fire zone of a following enemy ship and had become caught in the strange energy radiation. Under an instant annihilation of energy, the individual atomic structures of the alien craft immediately "caved-in" with an instantaneous compression of matter, and the entire structure of the huge mass was reduced in a twinkling to a supercontracted ball of heavy matter too small to be seen in the viewscreen.

Awed, Hedge said, "What the . . . ?"

"Terra 10 could become like same," Whaleman commented tensely. "Plus all humans aboard, compressed into a one-foot sphere. His glance flicked to Blue. "Report wave level."

"Level 16, and still building."

"Rosslin, report gunnery score!"

Forty-two targets destroyed, Gunner. Penetrations now negative. Sixteen targets remain in Zone Three defense, twenty-two in Zone Four, forty-six in Zone Five plus beyond."

"Good shooting," Whaleman snapped. "All AGRADs, depress to absolute range minimum. Lock-on steady fire. Core . . . give me Scale Maximum. Initiating tumble."

"It won't take Scale Max!" Hedge protested. "Not for more'n a few seconds!"

"Risk is necessary, gamble necessary, maybe we diffuse anti-energy buildup."

Hedge sighed and moved his controls to full range. The giant sphere began to tremble and throb, and once again went into polar rotation. All AGRAD batteries were sizzling continuously, the beams arcing together into the near-space surrounding the gunship. With polarities reversing furiously, the gleaming sphere's tumble was accelerating into a dizzying spin, as related to the targets in the viewscreens of the command cabin. Explosive energies were interacting along the outer edges of the shield, now spinning like a huge pinwheel, with tremendous ion clouds leaping into thousand-mile towers all about the gunship.

Hedge cried, "We're in Red Emergency!"

"Hold on Max!" Whaleman commanded.

Stel dropped to her knees beside Whaleman's chair, her eyes held hypnotically to the awe-inspiring scene on the screens.

Blue let out a happy squawk and exclaimed, "Level 0 and dropping!"

"Report arrival at Level 5!" the Gunner instructed him.

"We're tearing through! Level 8 . . . 7 . . . "

"Red Emergency Runaway!" Hedge yelled.

" . . . 6 . . . 5 . . . "

"Scale down to Core Optimum!" Whaleman commanded Hedge.

"Skronk!"

"Wave energies negative!" Blue cried triumphantly.

"AGRADs cease fire!"

Subgunner Rosslin immediately reported, "All targets receding."

"They're running out!" Tom Cole crowed. "They're turning tail and running!"

Whaleman was busily punching an interrogation into the master computer.

"All systems now optimum," he reported a moment later. "Prepare for wobble turn, starboard. Terra 10 also turns tail. This skirmish is ended."

"Skirmish?" an intercom voice gasped. "Hell . . . *skirmish*?"

"Subgunner, interrogate all guns. Institute automated maintenance program and standby. Blue, maintain vigil. Report any indications enemy regrouping."

Terra 10 was executing a sweeping turn across the galactic corridor and stabilizing into an easy tumble. A beeptone began sounding on the Command Communicator, and Whaleman moved quickly to admit the call.

"Well done, Terra 10," proclaimed a voice from Moonbase. "Andro Point Two reports, enemy in full retreat. Well done."

"All is not done," Whaleman murmured. He de-energized the communicator and spoke into the gunnery intercom. "Next battle line, Tom Cole, is Board Island."

"What's the plan, Zach?" Cole boomed back.

"Plan now is give Reevers voice at Board Island. What Director will not listen to Reevers now? This Reevercraft has saved Solana."

"I dunno," Blue murmured in mild protest. "For a Reever, Terra is still the land of the Boobs."

Whaleman smiled. "No, this is change now. Hedge, stand by for warp into solar envelope. Squadrons can now defend this slot."

"We're going back right now?" Stel inquired worriedly.

"Yes. Guns of Terra 10 talked for Solana. Now Solana must talk for man."

"I dunno," Blue repeated, rubbing his forehead. "We better keep these guns tuned up . . . just in case."

Hedge quietly reported, "Core is ready for supergrav lock-on."

"Skronk." Whaleman's fingers moved swiftly along the command buttons. "Coming up on warp out. Standby for corridor shift. Affirmative. We have warp."

"Warps," Blue sighed, "are the story of mankind."

CHAPTER TWENTY—ONE

The Fools

Squadroneer Mark Bond-Durant stepped out of the DDO and walked woodenly along the passageway toward the Chamber of Directors. A full scale Corporate Congress was in session, and his presence had been requested by the Defense Director. The Squadroneer knew the subject of discussion in that chamber—knew it and hated it—and he was making his approach in the manner of a man moving toward his doom.

He paused at an intersection and looked about him, as though expecting to see something which was not there. Then he heard the sounds of soft boots approaching along another corridor. He smiled and moved on to that intersection, arriving just as a large group of Defense Commanders trooped into view. One of the big men raised a hand in greeting.

"Ho, Squadroneer. Instructions?"

Bond-Durant replied, "Instructions like same earlier. Standby."

"Gunner Whaleman has arrived?"

"Soon. Standby and escort Gunner to chamber."

"Skronk."

The Squadroneer hesitated, flicking his eyes about in a quick count of the assembled troop, and said, "Twenty maybe is enough."

"More come," the Commander replied. "Maybe fifty total."

Bond-Durant nodded his head, went on along the passageway, and entered the chamber. This had been the scene of Whaleman's demonstration exercises of Terra 10's firepower . . . such a short time earlier, the Squadroneer was thinking. Such a triumph. Now—how much had changed.

The chamber was filled. The directors occupied a large circular table at the center. Managers and proxy-holders, numbering in the hundreds and representing all divisions of the Solan Corporation, were tiered in rings of ascending seats above and around the directors. Traditionally, the Chairman of the Board was represented by his communications automat which occupied a prominent place at the council table. Bond-Durant took a chair behind the Defense Director and sat at stiff attention.

An angry discussion was underway, with Johns-Fielding doing much of the speaking and his voice quivering with outrage.

" . . . and the official position of DDO is that this is a most shabby and shameful treatment for a hero of Solana. The DDO absolutely protests any motion toward a vote before Gunner Whaleman is given an opportunity to testify!"

The Chairman's automat whirred, "The DDO's protest is duly recorded and denied. Certification of proxies will now begin."

Johns-Fielding had turned panicky eyes toward his aide. Bond-Durant solemnly shook his head in a negative response to the unspoken question of those eyes. The Director spluttered, "I do not wish that my protest be merely recorded. The delay will be minimal. The Gunner is enroute to Board Island at this very moment."

"The DDO is out of order and is warned against further disruptive tactics. Certi—"

"Be *damned* with your warnings!" Johns-Fielding replied emotionally, shocking even himself. "DDO demands a poll of directors."

An uneasy stir at the council table greeted the Defense Director's outburst. The Chairman's automat whirred as its logic banks analyzed the request, then responded with, "Is there a second to the DDO's motion for a poll?"

A quiet voice from Johns-Fielding's right nervously said, "Technology seconds the motion for a poll of directors. Technology wishes to state an interest in the innovations in the Terra 10 command systems."

Another director half rose from his seat, noisily cleared his throat, and stated, "Personnel also wishes to record a seconding of the DDO motion. Personnel wishes to record an interest in the human systems recently incorporated into Terra 10."

Johns-Fielding shot a glance of relief and triumph to his aide. Bond-Durant smiled back and tipped his head in a silent salute. The Defense Director got to his feet and began the polling.

The vote came out eight to four in favor of delaying the indictment against Gunner Whaleman. The Director for Communications delivered a statement.

"Communications moves that the interim period be used for a discussion of the second telepic received from Andro Point Two."

Johns-Fielding snapped, "Defense seconds that motion," then he turned to Bond-Durant and whispered, "I forgot to tell you about that, Mark. We got a thirty-foot picture a short while ago, same source."

"Thirty *feet*?" the Squadroneer hissed.

Johns-Fielding nodded. "Quite involved, difficult to decipher. We believe it to be a history of their world, pictorialized, and an apology for the invasion. We were going over it when this idiotic business over Whaleman came up."

"*Idiotic* is not a word strong enough," Bond-Durant replied coldly. "Is treachery."

"Well don't worry. He's not going to get away

with it. He didn't have the guts to try it on his own. Thought he'd get a corporate indictment, called in all the proxies, tried to force a quick vote. He's slipping, the old man's slipping. He didn't count on all this adulation for Whaleman. I guess it's been a long time, Mark, since the human race had itself a full blown hero. The old man forgot how much power a—" He broke off and swung around quickly as the Chairman's automat began whirring into speech.

"Motion is denied. Discussion of telepic is not in order."

"The motion has been seconded," Johns-Fielding protested.

"The motion is out of order, invalid and therefore cannot be seconded. We will commence with the certification of proxies. Gunner Whaleman may be heard if he is present when certification has been completed."

The Defense Director was on his feet and shouting— "DDO maintains that a discussion of the second telepic from Andro Two *is* valid for this congress. The telepic bears directly on the incident involving Gunner Whaleman and is certainly pertinent to the subject of this congress."

"The Chair has ruled and the DDO is out of order."

"This entire corporation is out of order if a vote is even taken on this insane indictment of a man who saved our world from certain destruction! As for the telepic, the Chair is well aware of the content of that message. The attacking ships were sent by renegade elements bent on the destruction of all mankind, and perhaps even of all lifeforms everywhere. The actions of Gunner Whaleman and his valiant crew were the only impediment to those horrendous aims. Without these brave men, Mr. Chairman, there would be no

congress at Board Island at this time. There would
be no Board Island, Mr. Chairman—*and there
would be no Solan Corporation*! By what madness
do we punish the man who saved us all?"

A loud murmuring arose in the chamber,
drowning out the impotent clicks of the Chairman's automat. A loud screech erupted from the
instrument, signalling for order.

When quiet had been restored, the automat
whirred, "There is no question of the Gunner's
service to Solana, but the execution of this service
in no way provides an immunity against prosecu-
tion of insubordinate actions. The service was his
program, and entails no reward. The disservice,
direct insubordination to the Corporate Board,
does entail a penalty. Can the DDO guarantee that
further aberrant behavior by Gunner Whaleman
will always have such fortunate results? By what
madness, Mr. Director, does the Corporate Board
applaud reversionary characteristics in those programmed to defend the Solar System from its
enemies?"

"The Reevers saved us all!" Johns-Fielding
shouted. "Their feat has been unequalled by
hundreds of years of machine programming! Maybe what this old world *needs* is a bit of reversion
here and there."

"The Director of Defense will be removed
from the chamber!"

Bond-Durant leapt to his feet and towered
above Johns-Fielding. "Gunner Whaleman arrives!"
he announced dramatically, pivoting to sweep a
long arm toward the doorway.

The door swung wide to admit Whaleman and
his honor guard of defense commanders. They
moved silently into the chamber and proceeded
directly to the dais above the council table. The
fifty or so men of the honor guard quickly

arranged themselves into a formation resembling the defense command insignia, a pyramidal shield, with Whaleman standing stiffly at the apex.

A group of managers in the third section rose to their feet and began quietly applauding. Others quickly followed. Moments later, the Gunner was receiving a standing ovation from the assembled Corporate Body. He stood stoically accepting the thunderous applause. Long before it ended, however, the Chairman's security squadron began filing into the chamber from the Corporate quarters and gathered in a somber group behind the council table.

Even Johns-Fielding could not believe that which followed, especially in view of the reception accorded Whaleman by the Corporate Body. Before the applause had completely subsided, the automat was reading the charge against the Gunner—

"It is the decision of the Solan Corporation that the Defense Commander known as Gunner Zachary Whaleman be presented for disciplinary action, that he be stripped of all rank, decommissioned from the command, and remanded to the custody of the security squadron as an evolutionary revert. It shall be noted that the Board of Directors, by voice poll, have indicated a desire that the Gunner be allowed to answer this indictment. The Gunner may now make his statement."

Whaleman's eyes fell in dumb misery and disbelief to the tortured gaze of Ian Johns-Fielding.

"Does the Gunner wish to record a statement?" the automat whirred.

Whaleman's mouth opened and closed. His shoulders inclined forward in a tensely belligerent stance and a brief emotion flickered across his face.

"In name of humankind, Reevers must be freed," he stated in a choked voice.

"The Gunner's statement has been noted," the automat quickly replied. "He is now remanded to the custody of the Security Squadron."

Johns-Fielding again leapt to his feet. "This is outrageous!" he cried. "The Corporate Body has not yet voted on this indictment!"

"The vote is hereby ordered delayed for twenty-four hours, so that proxies may be recertified. In the meantime, Gunner Whaleman is remanded to custody. This congress is adjourned."

The men of the Chairman's special police began moving toward the dais. Bond-Durant stepped forward and violently shoved the leading policeman back. A brief scuffle ensued. A number of giant defense commanders leapt from the dais and took up a screening position. Bond-Durant broke contact with the police and joined the commanders at the base of the dais. The chamber was in an uproar. Johns-Fielding climbed onto his chair and wildly waved his arms, signaling for order.

"DDO will not allow this action to stand!" he roared.

The Chairman's police and the defense commanders were glowering at each other in a close confrontation. Whaleman raised his arms above his head and held them there. The noise of the chamber began to subside.

Johns-Fielding cried, "This is a mockery of Solan management. The Chairman of the Board of Directors does not hold sovereign powers." He looked at Whaleman. "Has the Gunner completed his statement?" he asked loudly.

"No," Whaleman said, his mind obviously struggling toward speech formation. "Statement has not begun. Zach does not defend insubordination indictment. Zach defends human spirit. Reevers are not incompetent, not childlike, not irresponsible. This is lie of centuries, carefully perpetu-

ated. Lies must end. Reevers are not *Reevers.*
Reevers are highest expression of human spirit.
These humans must be set free, must take place in
Solan society before too late, before last hope of
human spirit vanishes. This is statement. Proof is
like same, talking guns of Terra 10. This is
complete, this is statement."

The Director for Personnel was on his feet. He
cleared his throat with a harsh bark and said, "This
statement should be taken under advisement as a
separate issue, and Personnel hereby makes that
motion. Also, Personnel wishes to offer counsel to
the Gunner of Terra 10. It is your right, Gunner, to
personally confront your accuser. Who is the
accuser in the indictment of Gunner Whaleman?"
He had turned to the Chairman's automat.

The automat whirred a reply. "Let the record
show that the Gunner has been advised of his
rights."

"Who is the accuser?" the Personnel Director
persisted.

"The Corporate Body of Solana brings the
indictment," the automat replied. "The Gunner is
now facing his accusers."

"That's not true!" Johns-Fielding snapped. "A
Corporate vote has not been recorded. Let the
record show that the Chairman of the Board is the
accuser of Gunner Whaleman!"

"DDO is out of order," the automat whirred.

"This congress is out of order," Johns-Fielding
retorted. "Gunner, the Chairman is your accuser.
Ask your questions!"

"Is Chairman this automat?" Whaleman quietly
inquired.

Johns-Fielding's face dropped, then he smiled
brightly. "Good point, Gunner. Let the record
show that the Director for Defense assumes counsel for Gunner Whaleman. The Chairman of the

Board of Directors will now present himself in the chamber for interrogation.''

A reedy voice replaced the whirring tones of the automat. "Have you taken leave of your senses, Johns-Fielding? The Chairman may not show himself in the chamber!''

"Then these charges must be dropped,'' Johns-Fielding replied smugly. "Let the record show that the Gunner is publicly exonerated, no charge having been made.''

"No!'' Whaleman barked. "Gunner Whaleman *has* been charged. Let now this charge be answered.''

Johns-Fielding's face was creased in a baffled smile. "Well . . . I guess that's your right, Zach.''

"Get that man out of here,'' the reedy voice demanded. "The Congress stands adjourned.''

"No!'' Mark Bond-Durant cried. "This is true. Gunner has right to face accuser. As ranking military officer present, Squadroneer Bond-Durant declares for record this must stand. Will Chairman present himself, or will Defense Command assure his presence?''

The aged voice shrilled, "This is a military plot! The Security Squadron is ordered to defend the person of the Chairman of the Board!''

Bond-Durant was already signaling the defense commanders of the Whaleman honor guard. Outnumbering the police by four to one, they quickly neutralized that authority and hustled the policemen to the corridor. The Corporate Body within the chamber sat in frozen silence, perhaps aware that they were witnessing a startling moment of history.

Bond-Durant, Johns-Fielding and three commanders proceeded directly to the heavy door leading to the Corporate quarters, official sequestuary of the Chairman. Another brief scuffle ensued as they forced their way through the automated doorlocks.

Moments later, Bond-Durant reappeared, his face white and shaken. He stalked woodenly to the center of the council table, obviously stunned and laboring under a heavy emotion, raised a hand to rub his forehead, and said quietly, "Is true, Chairman cannot appear publicly. Apology, Chairman cannot appear." He lifted a hand toward Whaleman. "Zach, come. Confront accuser in Chairman's quarters."

Whaleman left the dais and moved slowly to his superior. Their eyes met and locked. Bond-Durant said, "Come," and whirled about and quickly returned through the shattered doorway.

Whaleman followed closely. The Squadroneer halted just inside the door and said, "Zach, prepare for shock."

He led the young Gunner on into the quarters and steered him into a glass-enclosed cubicle at the far side of a darkened room. Johns-Fielding and the three commanders stood in a quiet consultation alongside a turret of automats. Barely visible at the open end of the turret was the head of a high bed. Upon the bed lay a shriveled, barely human form. The wasted body was all but blanketed by a maze of electrodes, with a network of fine wires leading to the automat-turret surrounding the bed. The head was little more than a skull with a thin covering of practically transparent skin.

Whaleman flinched, then bent down for a closer look. Bloodless lips trembled and a reedy voice sighed, "Well, are you satisfied? Get out! Get out and leave me alone!"

"This is Chairman of Board?" Whaleman murmured.

The lips trembled again, but no sound issued through them.

Bond-Durant tugged Whaleman away. They joined Johns-Fielding who was interestedly inspecting the automats grouped about the bed.

"This is fantastic," the Director whispered. "Practically every biological function is being carried on by these robots. He's little more than a brain, and I suspect that the automats are largely supplementing even that. My God, no wonder we seldom hear his own voice. He couldn't have strength enough for more than a dozen words a day."

The Gunner and the Squadroneer began a close inspection of the machines. The Director for Personnel stepped into the room and went to the bed. His face blanched noticeably, and he hurriedly joined the others.

"Fools!" he hissed. "What fools we've been! And for how many years? When was the last time you saw the Chairman, Ian?"

Johns-Fielding miserably shook his head. "Never," he admitted. "Seventeen years on the board, and I never thought to question this setup."

"But it's been this way from beyond living memory," the other director muttered. "On what basis could we have questioned?"

"A one-man dynasty," Johns-Fielding commented, shaking his head.

Whaleman's technological genius had quickly deduced the function of the automated nurses.

"Correction," he murmured, "a machine dynasty. This Chairman is one percent human, ninety-nine percent machine. Is question now, which rules? The one percent, or the ninety-nine?"

Johns-Fielding sighed. "I guess we all know the answer to that, Zach."

"Yes, all know. Personnel Director says *fools?* This is true. Is question, for how long have machines ruled Solana?"

"That's not the question, Zach," Johns-Fielding replied. "The question now is *how much longer*. And I will presume to answer that question. The answer is, not another day, Zach. Not another minute."

"I'm going to bring the other directors in here," the Personnel man announced. "They all have to see this."

"All of Solana should see this," the Gunner angrily muttered. "All of humankind. Fools, yes. All fools. Are only Reevers fools, Director?"

"No, you're right, Zach. We're all fools. It's part of the human equation, isn't it. Only machines cannot be foolish."

The Gunner smiled faintly. "Is not so bad, this fools, Director. Is human. Is this fools restore Zach's faith in Solana. Reevers say Zach naive. Zach says, maybe so, but these fools naive also, like same. Zach speak to Board, for humankind. Board speaks back, these naive fools, speaking also for humankind with machine for Chairman."

"Zach, I don't know how to—"

"No, this is way of humankind. Sometime fool, sometime Godlike. This is good, Director. Is give hope for destiny of man."

The Personnel Director was returning, the balance of the Board filing in silently behind him.

Johns-Fielding sighed again. "Wait until you see the new telepic, Zach, then you'll see what fools we've *really* been."

"This concerns Reevers? Means they will be freed?"

"It could mean, Zach, that all mankind will be freed."

Whaleman grinned. "Free also to be fools?"

Johns-Fielding smiled wryly and nodded his head. "Yes, that, too. I guess that's as precious a freedom as any, isn't it?"

CHAPTER TWENTY-TWO

The Probabilities

Stel met him in the vehicle bay of Terra 10. They embraced, and the bubblingly happy girl told him, "We got the news on the communicators, Zach. It's so wonderful. Everything's going to be all right, now, isn't it?"

"Probabilities for this about sixty-forty affirmative," Whaleman replied. He wrapped an arm about her, and they trudged up to the command cabin.

Blue was seated at the master console, running through a dummy exercise with Hedge watching closely over his shoulder. Blue looked up at their entry and cried, "Hey, Boob! Home is the conquering warrior! Hey, I about got this thing figured out. Hedge, too. Give me a problem, any problem."

Whaleman grinned and replied, "Interrogate probabilities of Solani emigration to new world."

"I don't need to put that through an interrogator," Blue declared. "It's a matter of common sense. Seventeen billion people are just too many for one small planet to feed. I'd say there's going to be a—"

Laughing, Hedge broke in with, "See, Zach, he still don't trust the computer as much as his own hunches."

"Hunches maybe good also," the Gunner said. "Here is problem, Blue. Calculate probabilities two trained Reevers assigned lead design teams, new transports with propulsion system like same Terra 10."

"Huh?"

Whaleman's grin expanded. "Is true. Technology is request services. Fontainbleu/Oraskny and Hedges/Bolsom, new grav-lock program."

"Then I'd say it's the age of wonders," Blue marveled.

"Speaking of wonders," Stel said, laughing, "has any one noticed how much better Zach is talking?"

The Gunner colored somewhat and replied, "Zach promise learn speak social for Stel. Zach tries. Uh, where are Gunmen? Corporate Body wishes recognize publicly their service to Solana."

"Tom and Eva Rosslin took them back to 23," Hedge reported. "They were getting nervous cooped up in here."

Whaleman nodded understandingly. "New commission being formed," he told them, "Study integration of Reevers into Solan society. Meanwhile, gunmen are heroes, deserve recognition, must be presented to Corporate Body." He stepped over to the console and punched in a comm channel.

Bond-Durant's voice responded, "DDO."

"Gunner Whaleman here," the big commander reported. "Gunmen of Terra 10 have returned commune, AgSta 23, less Fontainbleu/Oraskny, Hedges/Bolsom, and Rogers/Brandt. Suggest contact them there."

"Skronk," came the reply. "What are your intentions? Do you remain aboard gunship?"

"Negative. Intentions are to marriage Stel."

Bond-Durant replied, "Unskronk."

The door to the command cabin had slid open during the exchange to admit Tom Cole and Subgunner Eva Rosslin, arm in arm.

Cole bellowed, "Tell 'im he better start skronking. Mars, man, there's liable to be marriages all over the place. Right, Eva girl?"

"This is correct, Tom Cole," the Subgunner replied, coloring furiously.

Whaleman chuckled. "This is good, like same,

human spirit soar to ends of universe, new horizons for mankind."

"Bet on that, spaceman, you just bet on it."

The puzzled voice of Bond-Durant came through the console. "Repeat your last, unskronk, unskronk."

Whaleman kissed his woman before replying, "This is new study for Personnel Director. Old human custom, maybe needs revival for new world colonies, maybe even old world. No program tracings, Squadroneer, just foolish human chances for excellence."

"Unskronk," Bond-Durant repeated.

Whaleman laughed out loud. "Request interrogate intelligence computer re: probabilities, marriage with Stel produce golden-hair Reevers versus redhair spacement."

"Unskronk, unskronk."

Blue snorted gleefully, "You don't need an intell—"

Stel cut him off, hugging Whaleman delightedly and crying, "I skronk that, Zach. I'd say the probabilities are about fifty-fifty."

"What is this fifty-fifty?"

The color of Stel's cheeks deepened. "Fifty of each."

The Gunner laughed heartily and propelled her toward the doorway. "Not here," he said, "not under guns of Terra 10. Religious waterfall, Stel, this is where."

"Yes," she breathed, her eyes glowing. "This is where. Probabilities are unlimited."

Hedge clapped his friend on the shoulder and the two of them bent their heads to the problems of the universe. Stel had been correct. The probabilities were indeed unlimited.

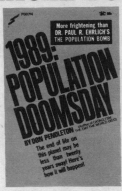